I0557710

LADY TWISDEN'S PICTURE PERFECT MATCH

ALINA K. FIELD

HAVENLOCK PRESS

Lady Twisden's Picture Perfect Match
© 2022 Mary J. Kozlowski

ISBN 978-1-944063-40-5

Havenlock Press

PO Box 1891

La Mirada, CA 90637

January 10, 2023

This is a work of fiction. Names, characters, places, and incidents either are the product of the author's imagination or are used fictitiously, and any resemblance to actual persons, living or dead, business establishments, events, or locales is entirely coincidental.

All rights reserved under International and Pan-American Copyright Conventions. No part of this text may be reproduced, transmitted, downloaded, decompiled, reverse engineered or stored in or introduced into any information storage and retrieval system, in any form or by any means, whether electronic or mechanical, now known or hereinafter invented without the express written permission of the copyright owner, except in the case of brief quotations embodied in critical articles and reviews.

The reverse engineering, uploading, and/or distributing of this book via the internet or via any other means without the permission of the copyright owner is illegal and punishable by law. Please purchase only authorized editions, and do not participate in or encourage electronic piracy of copyrighted materials. Your support of the author's rights is appreciated.

Cover design by Dar Albert of Wicked Smart Designs

Previously published in *Desperate Daughters, a Bluestocking Belles with Friends Collection.*

LADY TWISDEN'S PICTURE PERFECT MATCH

After years of tolerating her late husband's rowdy friends, Honoria, Lady Twisden, has escaped to York where she can paint, investigate antiquities, and enjoy her freedom. Then her stepson appears with a long-lost cousin in tow, the perfect image of an ancestor whose fierce portrait made her shiver with mad imaginings.

Promised York's marriage mart and the hospitality of his cousin's doddering stepmother, Major August Kellborn is shocked to find that his fetching hostess is the one woman who stirs his heart. To win her heart and hand, however, he must convince her he's not just a perfect image of his ancestor, but her perfect match.

Previously published in *Desperate Daughters, A Bluestocking Belles with Friends Collection.*

UNEXPECTED VISITORS

ST. HEDWIG'S PLACE, YORK

*H*onoria, Lady Twisden, accepted the stack of late mail from her housekeeper and reached for the teapot. After hours spent planning menus, writing letters, and posting her accounts, she'd finally sat down for a midday cup of tea.

"Thank you, Mrs. Dunscombe." She cleared her throat, wondering whether she ought to remark on the changing colors of the bruise the woman sported. The housekeeper had begged an afternoon off the week before to attend a meeting of like-minded reformers. The newssheets had filled columns reporting on the melee disrupting the gathering. Mrs. Dunscombe had fortunately not been taken up by the soldiers, nor, she claimed, had she participated in brawling. She'd merely run afoul of a forceful elbow in the terrible crush of the fleeing crowd.

Honoria had let the matter rest then, and she didn't wish to bring it up now. She'd had a difficult enough time convincing the hard-working woman to take this post. No sense in chiding Mrs. Dunscombe about her off-duty excursion when she herself had approved the half-holiday.

"Ye might as well hear it from me, my lady. Cook is fit to be tied. Found two more in a fresh sack of flour. Had to throw out the lot."

Honoria fought the urge to shudder. The mice of Twisden Manor had been her companions for fifteen years, but she *would not* share a home with their brethren in York.

"We need a cat. Find us a good mouser, Mrs. Dunscombe."

Here, at least there were no useless hounds to bedevil the cats. Ignoring the housekeeper's harrumph, Honoria picked up the stack of letters and studied them.

Perhaps *stack* was too lavish a term for this clutch of letters. There'd been more in the days before when her effort to embrace York society had paid off with a few invitations.

She shuffled through the current batch as she sipped her tea. Her mother-in-law's fat letter would be bulging with gossip about Harrogate, along with complaints about the taste of the medicinal waters there and her continuing lumbago. The Twisden steward had written as well—she prayed that Wes was not plaguing the man again about changes for the home farm.

If so, she was determined to not interfere. As the new lord of the manor, Wes must find his own way. She'd raised him to manhood, and trained him to be sensible, and though he had all the rosy-eyed exuberance of youth, she knew he would not overtax the estate budget by restocking his late father's kennels with a new, useless pack of hounds.

The third letter was addressed in a feminine hand she didn't recognize. Perhaps it was another invitation, one she'd be grateful for. Upon her arrival in York, she'd discovered that her main acquaintance here, her cousin, Rose, had taken herself off to Egypt —the lucky woman. How she envied Rose her ability to travel at will.

Still, she was happy to begin this adventure. She'd been delighted to encounter her niece, Patience, two Sundays in a row attending services at York Minster, and those the two high holy days, Palm Sunday and Easter. Patience had recognized her old Aunt Honoria, even though their last meeting had been at Honoria's wedding, when Patience was no more than a child. As it happened, Patience had moved into Rose's vacant home for the season, along with her flock of stepdaughters.

Honoria took a long drink of tea and set down the cup. "Please have Meg clear my dish here before our wee friends come up from the kitchen for a repast of crumbs. I'll read these in my study."

The housekeeper grunted and picked up a tray.

"I've set Meg to dusting upstairs, so I'll take your plate and your tea things. As to the cat business, milady, they bring their own sort of mess, Cook says, and she's not wrong. I'd liefer set out more traps." With a small head bob, the housekeeper departed.

Honoria rubbed the spot between her eyebrows where a headache threatened. Having her own home didn't mean she could have everything her own way, not if she wanted to have servants. Why on earth had Wes arranged such a large house for her? It was within her budget, but just barely. She needed enough help to keep dust and vermin at bay, and she couldn't afford to pay the sort of wages servants would demand of an autocrat. She'd try it Mrs. Duscombe's way.

After all, Honoria only had the lease until Midsummer, and then, fingers crossed, she and her maid, Olive Bixby, would leave England for more exploring.

She passed through into the drawing room and paused to survey her work, ready now for callers. The curtains had been shaken clean, the carpets beaten, and every scratched and faded surface of the Queen Anne pieces coated with beeswax. She'd labored alongside Mrs. Duncombe, and Meg, and Bixby, along with two young girls who came in as needed and went home at night to their families.

Lady of the manor she might have been, but she was no stranger to work. While Cook scoured the kitchen environs, Honoria and her crew had gone through the dining room and the two stately suites on the first floor, and the three smaller bedchambers on the second floor, and the small attic servants' rooms. Not that she was especially egalitarian—she simply wanted the task done, and as quickly as possible so she could get on with the true purpose of this repairing lease.

The faintest of rustles stirred the curtains and made her pause.

No. That had been merely the cool breeze. They'd cleaned away all temptation and closed up all the holes. They'd not seen any active vermin in this room, but the open window might tempt some in. She drew down the sash and stepped back.

It was as pleasant as a house could be for the five single women living there, four servants and their widowed mistress, all living without benefit of a *Male* presence to give them the sort of countenance her late husband would have mandated. The thought made her smile, savoring her independence, and she passed through to the hall.

Wes hadn't known about it, but the house had one room that called to her daily, the second-floor bedchamber that looked out on York Minster. She called it her study; it was really her studio. And her easel and paints beckoned her right now. Tomorrow was soon enough to begin seeing the sights of York.

As she crossed the battered black and white tiles of the hall, the knocker resounded.

Her blood spiked with a mix of apprehension and anticipation, and just a tad of annoyance. *She had callers.* Her painting must wait—and thank heavens they'd made the house presentable.

Meg was upstairs dusting. Mrs. Dunscombe was below stairs. Honoria smoothed her hair, ran her hands down the sides of her old day gown, and heaved the heavy door open.

"*Mother?*"

Wes was here, on her doorstep. Unexpected.

"Good heavens." She mustered a welcoming tone. "What a surprise."

"A pleasant one, I hope." A grin split his handsome face.

He had his father's blue eyes and dark blond hair, and none of his corpulence. She shoved the uncharitable thought aside and extended her hands.

He reached her first and lifted her, planting a kiss on her forehead, with all the exuberance of the six-year-old she'd taken into her heart.

Laughing, she told him to put her down.

"Why ever are you answering your own door?"

Here comes the scold. Having reached his majority and taken over the responsibility of the estate, the dear lad had begun trying to manage *her.* That was but one of the reasons she'd left Twisden Manor.

"Where is the footman? We need him to fetch in our trunks."

We?

Looking past the broad shoulder she saw another figure approaching and...

Good God. Heat swamped her and flamed in her cheeks. Dark eyes shot darts at her over a grimly set, thin-lipped mouth. The palpable sternness of Wes's companion sent a shiver of awareness through her. It was a familiar shiver, one she'd indulged during her tedious days at Twisden Manor when she'd found herself fighting off mad imaginings.

Wes's laughter shook her tongue loose. "My goodness, sir," she said. "You bear an uncanny resemblance to—"

"Old Ebenezer Twisden," Wes said. "Yes, it is as if the old Warden has come back to life, Mother. As soon as I laid eyes on him in Brampton, I knew he must be a relation. And do you know who he is, Mother?" He laughed again. "I've written to Granny to tell her. She'll be in alt when she reads the news."

A man of perhaps forty, he was about the same age as Wes's ancestor, the Warden in the painting at Twisden Hall who'd been in the King's service for many years when that portrait was done. This new incarnation of Ebenezer wasn't a particularly tall man, not as tall as Wes, but he still towered over her.

Old Ebenezer cleared his throat.

"But of course," Wes said. "Where are my manners? Mother, may I present my cousin, Major Augustus Kellborn. Gus, this is my dear stepmother, Lady Twisden."

While she curtsied, managing not to wobble, he dipped his head, never taking his gaze away.

Good holy heavens.

"We had a good meal at the last inn stop," Wes said, "but a cup of tea and a few biscuits wouldn't go amiss while the servants ready our rooms."

"Your rooms." She blinked. Wes expected her to take in him and this handsome cousin who made her skin tingle but... *There is no way.* This was her home. It was true that Wes had stepped in and helped her with the estate agent when he fussed about leasing the house to a widow living alone, but she'd made it clear to Wes that she paid the rent. He knew, too, that she wanted…needed some time away. She'd explained all that when she concocted this plan to spend the season in York.

Sighing, she led them into the drawing room. "I fear I have no spirits to offer you, but I can bring up some of my elderberry wine, or if you have a flask, you must feel free to imbibe. Make yourself comfortable and I shall return directly."

Fleeing the parlor, she paused on the backstairs, pressing a hand to her pounding heart. Augustus Kellborn was the stuff of every naughty dream she'd entertained about Ebenezer Twisden. Attired in his flowing dark wig, long coat, breeches and high boots, Ebenezer Twisden had pinned his gaze on her through countless dinners with Sir Melton and his endless stream of tiresome, rowdy guests. Long ago, Ebenezer had served one of the Border Wardens, rounding up rievers and imposing the Crown's law. Family legend said he was a fierce and brutal warrior. One could see it in his eyes.

She had, at first, been intimidated by Ebenezer's image, and then intrigued, and then she'd begun imagining the virile fighter stepping out of the painting and shoving his sword into Jeremiah Ripton's belly. Repeatedly.

One could see a similar strength of will in Major Kellborn, and she knew of his heroism from tales told by her mother-in-law.

What a ninny she'd been, and what a ninny she was being now. She'd give the men tea and the names of the best inns in York. Cousin to her late husband though he may be, Major Ebenezer could not give her household of women countenance, and she'd rather he took his skin-tingling, heart-hammering, cheek-heating virile male presence elsewhere. It would be harder to turn Wes away, but she must at least try.

2

THE VALIANT SIR SANCHO

Major August Kellborn, late of his Majesty's army, beat back an impulse to seize young Sir Westcott Twisden by the neckcloth and shake him.

He'd had long experience beating back that sort of urge with the young nodcocks he'd shaped into officers. He could do so now as well.

Gus paced to the window and looked out a sparkling clean pane onto the narrow street. Their traveling chaise wasn't visible, but Sir Sancho stood unaccompanied, busily watering a lamppost.

Gus had been in his cups the day he'd met Twisden at a horse market in Brampton, else he wouldn't have allowed the young pup the informality of his first name, respectable though Wes was. The malaise of his first long winter's sojourn at Whitlaw Grange, his new estate near what was once the Debatable Land, had made him more sociable than was his wont.

Still, he'd found the friendly lad more sensible than most his age, and the family connection had intrigued him. His late mother had written frequently about the Twisdens, the jovial late baronet and his amiable wife. He knew of their mutual ancestor, Sir Ebenezer Twisden as well, and so, he'd jumped at the chance to visit Twisden Hall. His very resemblance to the old warrior was astonishing, and Gus had been impressed with the well-run estate. Much of it the late baronet's sensible widow's doing, Gus's valet had learned.

And so, when Wes proposed visiting his stepmother and attending the York races and then sweetened the deal with the notion of a marriage mart—it had been a very long, lonely winter—Gus agreed to this sojourn in York.

He turned back to his young erstwhile host. "*Practically doddering*, you said."

Wes looked up from pouring spirits from a flask into a tumbler. "What?" His blue-eyed innocence was genuine. Wes saw his stepmother as an ancient, when she could scarcely be much beyond thirty. He ought to have paid more attention to his mother's descriptions of the Twisdens.

"I cannot stay under your stepmother's roof, Wes."

"Whyever not?"

"She is not by any means doddering. She's a widow, and one young enough that even with you here some of the time..." Wes had planned to depart for several days to visit his Grandmother in

11

Harrogate. "The presence of a single man in her household might stir gossip."

"She's three and thirty and is known to be very proper. Plus…" He glanced back at the closed door and lowered his voice. "Though she's clever and good, she's plain."

Gus gazed back at the now empty street. Perhaps plain was the right word to describe each of Lady Twisden's entirely unremarkable features. But taken as a whole, he would call her appearance amiable, moving, and in fact… pretty. The spark in her eyes when she spotted him, the color rising in her cheeks, those had stirred him as well.

Behind him the door opened, and nails pattered across the plank flooring and then hushed when they hit the carpet. Sir Sancho plopped at his feet.

"Took the liberty of letting himself in." Rompole, Gus's former batman and now valet stood in the doorway. "Tired of waiting on the footman. Ye did say yer ma wouldn't mind the mutt, Sir Wes."

Gus bent and patted the head of the brindled terrier. "Old boy, you and I will be finding an inn. Let us hope they'll allow us to share a room there."

"Nonsense," Wes said. "Why, at home, we had dogs in every room."

The door rattled and Lady Twisden poked in carrying a tray. A sturdily built woman of middling age sporting an apron and a bruised eye appeared behind her, equally laden.

To his credit, Wes jumped up, took the tray from his mother, and carried it to the large table near the other window. Rompole offered his assistance to the puckered-up servant who scowled through her fading bruise and ignored him.

Lady Twisden turned from directing the trays and her gaze settled on Gus's boots. Or rather, on Sir Sancho, who sat squirming and attempting to wag the tail he was sitting on.

"A dog." The words floated out on a low breath that might have been a sigh of relief but was more likely a squelched growl.

"Meet Sir Sancho, Mother." Wes made introductions, blissfully unaware of the lady's reaction. "Gus's Spanish terrier. He's learned English now though, haven't you Sir Sancho. Attached himself to my cousin and came all the way from Spain. I say, Mother, do you plan to pour?"

She ignored him, piercing the dog with a look that was anything but amiable. Lady Twisden had depths.

For his part, Sancho appeared smitten. He faced the lady, dancing from one forefoot to the other, his rump bouncing on his wriggling tail.

Gus swallowed a chuckle. The loyal dog had never displayed such ardent discomposure before, not even when tempted by food. And *now* he would play the faithless cur. "He wishes to greet you, my lady."

She blinked and leveled a prim look at both master and beast. "After which he may go out to the garden. Come, Sancho."

When she extended her hand, the dog—*his* dog—

trotted over to her, sat, and lifted a paw. She took it and shook, and Sancho licked her hand.

Rompole let out a breath through his teeth and muttered, "Well I'll be."

"Oh-ho," Wes said. "Well-mannered, isn't he, Mother? Go ahead and get to know him while I pour. You won't want to send him to the stable after you've made his proper acquaintance."

"I don't have a stable," the lady said.

Wes froze with the teapot in hand and frowned. "Dash it all, no you don't. We'll have to find a place for our horses, Gus." He turned on the other woman. "You, ma'am, could you send one of the footmen—"

"This is my housekeeper, Mrs. Dunscombe," Lady Twisden said, releasing Sancho's paw. "And I don't employ a footman, Wes."

Gus signaled his valet. "My man, Rompole, here, will accompany Sancho to the garden. And then I will take both horses along and see to their stabling. We'll find an inn to accommodate all of us."

* * *

Honoria let out a sigh of relief. Major Ebenezer was an insightful gentleman. As was his dog, so far, though the animal was making no effort to leave with the servant.

"*What?* No, Cousin," Wes cried. "You don't mean to go to an inn when you could reside here in comfort with family. We've come for the races, Mother, and for a bit of society. You wrote, did you not, that your niece is here with a houseful of marriageable daughters." He winked at her. "Gus is an eligible bachelor, you know."

"As are you, dear one." She winked back at him. "I fear, though, that you both might find an inn more comfortable than the home of a widow with only a few servants."

"Hire more." Wes waved his hand and then handed the Major a sloshing cup.

She intercepted the cup and returned it. "Sit down, Wes. I will take over the pouring. Major?"

"Milk only, my lady, and thank you." With the slightest of smiles he accepted the fresh cup and a plate with a slice of seedy cake—still warm from the oven as it was the dessert for the evening's meal, hastily coopted for these unexpected guests.

His lips had quirked like that when the dog sought her out, a flash of humor that made her wonder if he'd trained his terrier to beguile reluctant ladies. Sir Melton would have loved such a trick if he'd bothered to train his slobbery hounds to do anything else but track scent.

When she took her seat, the dog settled down at her feet, remarkably well-behaved and seemingly not at all interested in her plate. Sir Melton's hounds would have been atop the table by now, lapping up everything except the hot tea. Perhaps Spanish terriers were better bred than their English cousins, or else the vicissitudes of war had taught the dog manners.

"I'll go to the agency myself and find you some footmen," Wes said.

She carefully sipped, holding back her first instinct to scold. Wes was a man, and she must treat him as such, especially in front of an older cousin he admired.

Before she could form a response, the major stood. "Please excuse me, but I can't keep the postilion waiting. Rompole will fetch your trunk into the house, Wes, and we'll be on our way."

The servant, who like Dunscombe was somehow still in the parlor with them, shuffled his feet like the dog had done earlier. "Er, Major, I already carried in both trunks. Untied the horses and found a boy to watch them. Chaise has gone off to the posting inn. The lad said he couldn't wait."

"There. You see, Mother? Rompole has settled everything for us." Wes flung out a hand and the crumble of cake he was holding flew toward the window.

The terrier alerted and shot after it.

So, Spanish terriers were not so decorous. Only a bit better behaved than Sir Melton's—

A loud squeak from the corner preceded a vigorous shaking. Sancho returned, dropped a bundle of fur near her toes and ran off again.

Her blood surged and drained, and she heard a squeal—her own—and a startled huff and found Mrs. Dunscombe peering over her shoulder. Sancho shook violently and returned twice more. Three fat mice lay at her feet, not even twitching.

"Better'n a cat," Mrs. Dunscombe whispered. "I'll get the shovel."

"Rompole will see to the, er, removal," the major said. "Apologies, my lady. Sancho is a fierce ratter. I fear I haven't been able to train him to restrain his natural instincts."

Honoria looked at the pile of dead rodents then nodded to Dunscombe. "Ask Meg to ready the first-floor bedchamber for Sir Westcott and the front bedchamber on the second floor for Major Kellborn." She broke off a piece of biscuit and let Sancho nibble it from her hand. "Well done, Sir Sancho. Well done, indeed."

"You won't regret the company, Mother."

Wes had joined her in the parlor for a much-needed talk before Major Kellborn came down for dinner. Outside, the sounds of horses clopping and wheels clattering signaled a busy time of day in this neighborhood of tradesmen and professional men.

All at his leisure, Wes leaned back in his chair and crossed one leg over the other. "And we have Sir Sancho to thank for convincing Gus to stay."

The thought of the dog had her shaking her head and chuckling. That wee bit of fur had been resolute, sitting like a statue at her feet and refusing to heed his master's call. To his credit, Major Kellborn had taken the betrayal in stride. Accepting the dog's fickleness with good grace, he'd turned his back on Sir Sancho and followed Wes and his valet upstairs.

Once the major left, Sir Sancho rose immediately at Honoria's command and allowed her to escort him to the kitchen. Upon his arrival there, he'd headed straight for the larder and gone to work at once, forestalling any objections by Cook. In fact, he'd won her over so completely that she barely fussed at the necessary menu changes and extra mouths to feed.

After, Honoria had retired to her own bedchamber to change for dinner and bend Bixby's patient ear fretting over stretching the budget. There'd been room in her budget—just barely—to help Patience with funds for the fête she was hosting at Smithfield's Assembly Rooms on the twenty-second of the month. The proposed ball was, after all, a noble endeavor, meant to help each of the young Bigglesworth ladies find a worthy husband. Why, even Patience, who was lovely and such a young widow, only two and twenty, might marry again.

The Bigglesworth stepdaughters ranged in age from thirty to Patience's only daughter by Seahaven, her three-year-old. There were five—or perhaps six —of an age to marry. Patience's greatest hopes were for a stepdaughter, aged nineteen, and a set of eighteen-year-old twins who all had been deemed diamonds of the first water.

Poor Patience! What a responsibility. The arrangement of Honoria's marriage to Sir Melton had been a near thing, given the puny size of her dowry. At eighteen, she hadn't been quite desperate to marry, but with her parents' health failing and her sister's disgrace, a practical marriage had seemed prudent. She would have wished for love, though.

It was too late for Honoria, but the Bigglesworth girls ought to have a chance at more than practicality. Perhaps one of the young ladies would be a good match for Major Kellborn or even Wes. Though Honoria couldn't imagine her stepson being ready just yet to settle down into matrimony.

Right now, she and Wes needed to discuss money, a topic both vulgar and necessary. In the old days, before he'd reached his majority, she would have spoken quite forthrightly, and he would have paid respectful heed to her concerns. But since needing to seek his help with the leasing agent, she was finding this new Wes a bit too high-handed.

"I wonder if we may dragoon the Major's man for some of the duties we might otherwise bestow on a footman?" she mused. "You know, it may be a challenge to find a man for a position that will end in a matter of weeks. In fact, I had difficulty engaging a housekeeper and Cook. And, well, to be perfectly honest, Wes, as I have always tried to be, not wishing to be a burden to you..." She took in a breath and framed her words. "I've carefully budgeted for my future travels."

He slapped his leg. "Is that it, old dear?"

The condescending endearment had her bristling, and she clamped her right hand firmly with the left, else it might fly out and slap him. "*Old dear?*" she asked, managing to keep her tone even.

He laughed. "Dear Mother. You have only to ask.

I'll foot the wages for a couple of men." He straightened and snapped his fingers. "And the wine bill shall be mine, and anything extra your cook will need, as we certainly want to make our illustrious war hero comfortable."

Major Kellborn did not seem to be a peacock, and she rather doubted he thought of himself as either illustrious or a war hero. In fact, it seemed possible such accolades would make him uncomfortable.

Though Major Kellborn's name had rarely been mentioned in the dispatches published in the Yorkshire Post, her mother-in-law, a prodigious letter-writer, had followed his military career through her many correspondents, and with a great deal of pride. After all, Major Kellborn's late mother had a been a cousin of Wes's grandfather, and a dear friend to the dowager Lady Twisden.

"You may as well pay a visit to your grandmama at Harrogate," Honoria said. *And take Major Kellborn with you.*

"I plan to."

"And when he does, Lady Twisden, I shall remove myself to an inn." Major Kellborn had appeared in the doorway, quite earlier than expected. He'd changed out of his tight-fitting dusty buckskins and coats and attired himself in dark coat and trousers and a brocaded but tasteful waistcoat. He looked every bit the gentleman, and not a provincial one, but one who'd traveled in the best society.

She was glad she'd worn her best gown, a blue

sarsenet she'd had made when she came out of mourning.

"Sancho may of course, stay in service to you, my lady." Major Kellborn's lips didn't curve up, but his eyes twinkled.

Wes sprang out of his seat. "You must come with me to Harrogate, Gus. You must meet my grandmother. She's followed your military career as avidly as if you were her own son. The young ladies can wait a few days to fawn over a war hero."

The major dipped his head, almost hiding the grimace. She'd been right—he was uncomfortable with the attention.

And perhaps it had to do with the age of this elderly admirer. He might not grimace over accolades from the younger ladies. She must see if any of Patience's girls had a yen for a military man.

A distant knock sounded—the door knocker.

3

ANOTHER UNEXPECTED
VISITOR ARRIVES

*W*hat now? "It's an odd time to call," she said, rising. Mrs. Duncombe was busy with dinner preparations. Meg and Bixby were below stairs helping as well, and the major's man had gone out to tend to some business involving the men's horses.

"Be seated, Mother." Wes strode to the door, looked back over his shoulder, and grinned. "I'll play footman."

The major watched him leave and then turned back to her. "I truly don't wish to impose on you."

"You are not," she lied. "And the dog *is* very helpful."

He did smile then, eyes crinkling, lips turning up in a way that made her almost feel giddy. "I've grown very attached to the little cur, but I fear we must part ways. Sancho has chosen you."

"Oh, no, of course I cannot—"

"He'll give you no option. He chose me the same

way, just walked away from his last master and never looked back."

"No." She shook her head. "You must take him with you when you return home. I'm only in York for the quarter. And after that, I plan to… to travel."

He smiled again. "Sancho is a good traveler, as long as there are no boats involved. Will there be boats?"

Before she could answer, the door opened, and Wes waved an arm with a flourish. "Look who is here, Mother." A wizened lady with twinkling blue eyes entered.

It just needed this. Her mother-in-law had arrived.

The lady went right up to the major and reached for him. "Augustus Kellborn. When Westcott wrote I knew I must come and join you. What a pleasure to see you again."

Honoria may as well turn the house over to all of them and go to an inn herself. Oh, but then she wouldn't have her glorious view of the Minster and she wouldn't be able to *finally* finish a painting.

GUS RESTED HIS SPOON AND PATIENTLY ANSWERED THE dowager's umpteenth question about his new estate in Cumberland. He'd inherited Whitlaw Grange from a childless relation, and after his first winter there, he understood why the man never married. It was a fine house for a man who liked hunting, fishing, and Roman history, but where a lady was concerned, not even the well-maintained manor house with its modern conveniences could compensate for the remoteness of the location.

They talked about mutual family members as well, Wes's grandmother providing more details than he could. He'd been both gone for many years *and* a poor correspondent. But when she ventured into his military career, he parsed his words, and carefully avoided wincing at memories he'd sooner not discuss.

"Was Talavera as frightful as the papers reported?" The dowager Lady Twisden paused her spoon over the custard. "No, do not say a word. I know it must have been, and you don't want to speak of it. And besides, Honoria is sending me that *look*."

Honoria. Gus gazed down the table at the other Lady Twisden, Gus's stepmother. *Honoria*—what a pretentious name for such a down-to-earth lady. She ought to have a pet name—Nora, or perhaps Honey, like the color of her hair. Yes, Honey would be better, as she was smiling, a sweet and genuine smile, directed at her mother-in-law.

She'd taken her mother-in-law's arrival with amazing grace—after barely a flutter of her eyelids and a momentarily rise in her color, she'd embraced the older lady and ushered her upstairs to change out of her dusty carriage gown.

Following that, she must have gone below stairs and cast whatever spell had been needed upon the meager group of underpaid—if he was to believe Wes

—servants so that they were able to sit down to dinner only a quarter hour later than planned.

Now, Gus sent her a grateful nod and turned to the dowager. "My mother always spoke fondly of you, my lady. Perhaps tomorrow when we are both rested from our travels, I may answer all those questions about Spain."

"Oh, dear boy, you must not *my lady* me. You may call me Cousin Genny, as your mother did."

He dipped his head. "And you may call me Gus, Cousin Genny, as Wes does." He held his breath, wondering if Wes's stepmother would allow him the intimacy of using her Christian name—the formal one, Honoria. He would save pet names for a closer acquaintance.

And a closer acquaintance there would be. She was just the sort of lady for him. On the practical level, she knew how to thrive in the country, but wasn't averse to getting away and traveling.

But when she smiled at him and her color rose, practicalities weren't foremost on his mind.

"What are your plans for your stay in York?" the dowager asked.

"Why, we're here for the races, Grandmama," Wes said. "They're not for a few weeks, but we shall find ways to keep occupied until then. I should like to visit some of the stud farms in the area. Find a spare for my stable." He lifted a hand. "Nothing extravagant, Mother."

"And you, Honoria? Have you called on your niece?"

"Yes, I have, and we've met at a few social events. It's been a whirlwind getting the house sorted, but I intend to call on her often now that we are both more settled."

"Whatever will you do with the rest of your time, Mother?"

The lady sat up straighter, hiding what was must certainly be an urge to bristle at her impudent stepson's tone.

"There's a great deal of society in York," Honoria said, her cheeks tinging a lovely shade of pink. "I've made the acquaintance of Lady Clune, and through her I've received invitations. For the inquiring mind, there's much to see in York, a great deal of Roman history."

Her eyes brightened at the mention of Roman history, and he was delighted to see they had a common interest to pursue while he pursued her.

She tipped her head and went on. "The York Antiquarian Society is quite active. I've been introduced to the director, Mr. Herbert Nedhelm, and his wife. And there's to be a guest lecture by a visiting scholar, Dr. Malcolm Marr, who will speak on ancient Egyptian medicine."

The mention of Marr drew him out of his romantic strategizing.

"Would that be Malcolm Marr, Strathnaver's younger brother?" he asked.

"Yes." Cousin Genny nodded. "I believe so. Is he not a particular friend of yours, Gus?"

"Since Eton," he said. "I'll look forward to attending his lecture."

Wes laughed. "Roman history and Egyptian medicine. What else do you plan to do here, Mother?"

"Now that she's turned you loose to run Twisden Manor, Wes, she'll be painting, will you not, Honoria?" the dowager asked.

Color rose higher in the younger lady's cheeks.

"Honoria was run ragged by that son of mine, Gus. She had little time to pursue her own interests. Not that Melton thought ladies should have their own interests."

"Drawing pictures of old buildings," Wes muttered.

"I am sure," Cousin Genny said, "that we might find you a better drawing instructor in a city as big as York. Wes had a drawing instructor for a time, Gus, but I believe Honoria learned more from the lessons. You will see, Honoria, with help and practice, how much your work improves."

"Oh yes." Honoria picked up her glass, her cheeks now the same rosy hue as the wine. "What think you of this claret, gentlemen?"

Cousin Genny waved a hand. "I can see they've both had their glasses refilled, Honoria. Now, you must tell me more about your visit to Farnley Hall. Was Turner there?"

"Turner?" Wes said. "You visited Turner, Mother? By yourself?"

The flush in Honoria's cheeks poured down into her modest decolletage. A yearning to see how far the pink flowed warred with an urge send Wes's chair flying.

Had Gus stayed at an inn, he wouldn't have stumbled across this sort of family tableau. Though Honoria was no blood relative of either of the Twisdens, the family was close. Only one's beloved relations could inflict such embarrassment.

Aside from the color in her cheeks, Honoria held her composure. Gus stayed all his yearning and urges, curious to hear how she answered.

"I stopped with Bixby at Farnley Hall when I was passing through Otley. The housekeeper was most kind, and no, Mr. Turner was not visiting, nor was Mr. Fawkes in residence, else I wouldn't have imposed."

The mention of Fawkes jiggled Gus's memory. "Would that be J.M.W. Turner?" he asked. How would a lady residing in rural Westmoreland be knowledgeable of *that* Turner? "I saw some of his watercolors in London."

Her eyes lit. "I have never visited London, but the art tutor had. I've read of his work, and I was able to see some of his sketches and paintings at Farnley Hall. I admire his technique. What did *you* think of the paintings you saw, sir?"

Gus heard a note of challenge and groped for words. The man's landscapes and seascapes were certainly dramatic.

She shook her head. "I suppose they're not to everyone's taste. My late husband was not fond of art either, unless the subject was hunting or dogs." She turned a strained smile on Wes. "To answer your earlier question, I do intend to paint, but as I said, there is much history to explore in York, and I intend to see it all. This is, after all, an ancient city. Constantine was proclaimed emperor of Rome by his men here. In fact, I plan to begin my exploring tomorrow."

Wes sighed. "It would be indiscreet for you to go exploring on your own. You must wait until the day after when I am free." He signaled for more wine, and the rail-thin woman serving them strolled over. "Thank you, Bixby," Wes said. "Tomorrow, you shall not have to perform footman duty. I'll be visiting the agencies in the morning to bring in more help."

"Bixby will accompany me tomorrow, Wes. Major Kellborn, this is my maid, Olive Bixby, who has been kind enough to serve us tonight. Do not worry, Wes. I'll leave my jewels and my piles of gold at home. We two older ladies shall be perfectly safe walking the city walls and exploring the Shambles."

Bixby looked unconvinced and kept her mouth closed as Rompole would not have done. Wes, an equally imprudent male, opened his mouth. "Mother..." He cleared his throat, preparing a pompous objection. More sensible than many young men who'd just inherited Wes was, but he hadn't yet learned how to wield his new power tactfully, especially where this kind lady was concerned.

"I should like to accompany you, Lady Twisden," Gus said. "If you'll allow it."

"You'll find yourself stopping at every shop," Wes said, "and no footman to carry the packages."

Honoria sent her stepson a bland look before bestowing a polite smile on Gus. "Of course, you may join us, Major Kellborn. I daresay you'll find us tiresome, and then you may make your excuses with a clear conscience and search out a pint of ale."

Her hair shimmered in the candlelight, and though she held his gaze, her lower lip quivered just enough to tell him she was either nervous or amused. He would never find this lady tiresome.

She turned that bright smile on Wes. "As for you, dear boy, since you'll be free the day after tomorrow, you and I shall pay a call on my niece, Patience, Lady Seahaven, and her young ladies."

Wes sighed. "Of course. Are they pretty, these young ladies? I hope they are at least pretty."

"What a question," Honoria exclaimed. "I can safely say that I've seen all the girls, and Patience and her stepdaughters are all very comely. But remember, beauty is in the eye—or perhaps the heart—of the beholder, as I have always told you."

Cousin Genny clapped her hands. "Well said, Honoria."

"Indeed," Gus said, sending the lady a long look. "I have always found that to be true."

Cousin Genny grasped her grandson's hand. "It's what I ought to have told your father when he was your age, Wes. Your mother, God rest her soul, was too pretty for her own good. But the poor lass had not an ounce of sense."

"Are the Bigglesworth girls spirited, Mother?" Wes asked. "I cannot abide a melancholy girl, no matter how much beauty. That was my own mother's problem, wasn't it, Grandmama? She wasn't lacking in sense; she was just too gloomy. Father always told me it was my stepmother's spirit that convinced him to marry her."

"Your stepmother isn't spirited, you goose. She's sensible and stubborn, as she had to be living with my son in the middle of nowhere."

Gus cleared his throat, sensing Honoria's discomfort. She was studying her dish of half-finished custard. "And sensible stubbornness is a mark in any lady's favor," he said.

When she looked up, he couldn't read her expression. "I shall not require you to join us in calling on my niece, Major. However, Patience is hosting a ball several days from now at the Smithfield Assembly Rooms, and I shall impose on both of you to attend the ball. In fact, I'm one of the sponsors for this event, and I intend for it to be a great success. Patience is a very young widow, only two-and-twenty, with several marriageable stepdaughters. I'm not asking either of you to choose a bride, though how wonderful if... Well in any case, I require you to dance with each of the young ladies, and Patience, as well."

Cousin Genny chuckled. "Westcott, I'll join with Honoria pushing you onto the dance floor. Cousin Gus, will you be so gallant as to dance with the young ladies?"

Gus tapped the table and furrowed his brow, pretending to think about the question. He sent his hostess his most imperious look, the one that set all the raw recruits shaking.

She blinked, and then held his gaze steadily. There was a world of patience in the woman.

"I shall do it," he said. "On one condition. Lady Twisden, Honoria, you must allow me two dances with *you*."

Wes laughed. "Mother don't dance."

She blinked again, shuttering a flash of irritation. "I may be a bit rusty, but if you will risk some embarrassment and your toes, I agree to your terms, Major."

"Never saw you stand up at a party," Wes said. "Always pushing the young girls out onto the floor. Why, only last month, Ripton was complaining that you'd always…" He sat up straighter. "Why, Mother, Ripton is coming to York. He must have arrived by now, and I know he'll call on you soon." He turned back to Gus. "Jeremiah Ripton is local gentry, a good friend of my father."

"I am sure, Wes, that it's you he wishes to see," Honoria said. "Best meet him over a pint somewhere."

"Of course, he'll call on you, Mother, especially now that both of you are widowed."

She grimaced and signaled the maid. "Mother Twisden, shall we leave the two gentlemen to their spirits and withdraw to the parlor?"

"Yes," Cousin Genny said. "But I'll retire to my

room. I have letters to write. Bixby, ring for Jones, please. She must be finished moving Honoria's things by now."

"I'll help you up," Honoria said. "In fact, I believe I'll retire as well. Gentlemen, why not have your sherry in the parlor and turn in whenever you wish?"

Both ladies and the maid departed, leaving him with Wes.

This was certainly not the respite from Cumberland he'd expected. He'd thought to come to York to attend the races, take part in society, and perhaps... perhaps meet a lady he might want to marry, all from the sedate comfort of the doddering widow's guest bedchamber.

And he found it was the widow he wanted.

Wes clapped him on the shoulder. "I hear that the taproom at the Golden Fleece is favored by some of the sporting men. What say you we have our nightcap there?"

A maid—a younger girl than the other—entered and curtsied. Wes sent her to fetch their hats, and within minutes, they set off walking.

4

AN EVENING AT THE GOLDEN FLEECE

A mixture of gentlemen and tradesmen glanced up at the new arrivals entering the Golden Fleece's busy taproom. Gus and Wes had barely found seats at one of the tables crowding a back corner when Wes lifted a hand and signaled a man across the room.

The fellow rose and came to join them. Of an age with Gus, he was what the ladies would call handsome: fit and with a full head of curls, a square jaw, and gleaming teeth. He also wore a smug certainty about him that Gus instantly distrusted.

"Twisden," he exclaimed, "well-met."

Wes made introductions. The new arrival was Jeremiah Ripton.

Ripton waggled his eyebrows. "How is your lovely stepmother?"

"Fit as a fiddle and all settled in."

Gus's blood heated. The waggling eyebrows, the

leer… the oaf's intentions toward Honoria were clear. Her nodcock of a stepson didn't see it.

Now he understood her reaction to the man's name at dinner. She was too sensible and intelligent not to see through this lout. The urge to grab Ripton by the neckcloth was almost overpowering. But he restrained himself; he'd learned self-control in hard schools.

Wes called an order to the barmaid. "Where are you staying, Ripton? I daresay Mother might have a spare chamber for an old friend of my father's."

Gus raised an eyebrow at him.

"No." Wes laughed. "You're right, Gus. I had best ask her first. Gus, here, may have taken the last free bedchamber, but of course, you understand, Ripton, Gus is family."

And he would never remove himself to an inn if there was any danger of Ripton taking his vacated bed.

He held his tongue on that subject and joined the discussion about hunting and dogs—Ripton had bought out most of the late baronet's kennels.

"What of you, Kellborn?" Ripton asked. "Do you hunt?"

"Gus's only dog is a ratter," Wes said. "A damn fine one. He's won over Mother."

Ripton's gaze narrowed. "You've won the lady over with a dog?"

Gus smiled benignly, aware that he was stirring the man's jealousy. Ripton clearly thought he himself had a claim on Honoria.

Wes slapped the table. "The dog has won her over, Ripton. Took to her right off and plopped three fat mice at her feet." He laughed. "Dead of course."

Ripton's answering chuckle was false. "One more round," Gus said, signaling the maid and then changing the subject to the favorites for the upcoming races. Ripton was a man who crowed about his wins and never mentioned a loss. He was the smartest judge of horse flesh in Westmoreland.

Whoever Ripton claimed to be going for, Gus would bet against.

"THIS IS THE BEST YOU COULD DO FOR YOUR stepmother?" Ripton asked.

They'd paused in front of Honoria's townhouse. The ass had joined Gus and Wes for the walk home, no doubt angling to see where Honoria lived so he could prey on her another day.

"Best I could do?" Wes said. "Why, Mother would have taken two rooms in a boarding house if I'd let her have her way. *No fuss*, she said. But I couldn't allow that. She's plump enough for better quarters."

Rompole yanked the door open before Ripton could open his damned mouth again.

"Good of your man to play porter," Wes said.

Ripton sized up the burly valet, slid a glance Gus's way, and then wished them a good night.

Gus watched him leave, wondering when he'd have the opportunity to plant him a facer. When he turned back to his valet, Rompole was frowning at the back of Ripton's coat.

"Thank you, Rompole," Gus said, handing over his hat. His man was the sort to know where he was needed. It was why Gus tolerated his less than refined qualities. Well, that and the way he could shine up the foulest boots.

Gus followed his host up the stairs.

At the landing, Wes paused at a door, frowning. "I unpacked a tolerable bottle of brandy. Join me?"

The door led to a sitting room, and beyond that the bedchamber.

"Spacious, isn't it?" Wes asked, pouring a glass. "Mother's is equally large, or so the estate agent said." He handed over a glass. "Or was. She's given over the room to Grandmama. I don't know where she's moved."

"At least *I* haven't displaced her."

Wes waved a hand. "Oh, Mother don't mind. She has plenty of money if she don't follow through on her harebrained plan to go off to Scarborough and paint the sea. She ought to come home to Twisden Manor and paint the brook if that's how she wants to fritter away her time. What think you of Ripton? He's been after her for years—I shouldn't know that, but I do. Mother would never have anything to do with him, even after Father died. Of course, Ripton's wife was still living then. Honorable of Mother, but now that Ripton's lady has passed, I believe we could bring him up to scratch with my mother and have a guarantee of keeping her close to home. Will you help me?"

His hand had tightened around the squat glass, his throat going dry. Ripton and Honoria? The notion was appalling.

Gus eased his grip, drained his glass, and said, "No."

"She's lonely." Wes went on as if he hadn't heard. "It would set her up fine, and our man would make sure she had a respectable dower. I thought to ask for a pair of the hounds back as part of the settlement."

He reached for the bottle and topped off his glass. Poor Honoria.

Not even a forty-two pounder could dislodge Gus now. He'd well and truly remain here between this young ass and the old one he'd met at the Golden Fleece. If Honoria wanted to travel and paint and had the funds to do so, why shouldn't she?

Maybe he should go with her.

"Ripton is not interested in *marrying* your stepmother, Wes," he said. "You said yourself, he's been after her since before both your father's death and his wife's. I've known many men like him. Let me say this plainly: he wants to bed her."

As do I.

Wes's head jerked up and his color rose, and for a moment he wondered if he'd expressed his own interest out loud.

Never mind. "Your friend, Ripton is a sporting man who likes to win. He's taken your mother's refusal as a challenge, that is all. I know you care for her. It would be unkind of you to have her think he's planning marriage."

He left the lad sitting speechless and took the flight of stairs up to the next floor. A dim lamp illuminated four doors in the corridor. Light seeped under two of them, his own and the one across from his.

A soft scrabbling and a woman's chuckle made him pause with his hand on the latch. The sound came from the room across from his.

"*Now* you need to go out?"

The door opened and Sancho bounded out, pouncing on him. He bent to rub the dog's ears and when he straightened, his breath caught. Honoria stood in the doorway, her robe open over a filmy night gown, her unbound hair cascading about her shoulders.

HONORIA FROZE IN PLACE, AS SPEECHLESS AS THE MAN trailing his gaze over her deshabille with the same haughty arrogance as Sir Ebenezer.

Well, perhaps there was more heat in the Major's eyes, and it was stirring an answering sensation in the pit of her belly. Or, at least in that vicinity.

How odd. She shook off her paralysis. "He's decided to go back to you, I think." She stepped back and pushed the door.

Before she could close it, Sancho darted back into

the room and disappeared under the tester bed, his collar medallion rattling on the plank floor.

She scoffed. "Brazen fellow."

"He was just greeting me." The deep baritone sent ripples along her skin. "He knows I'm just, er, here."

Yes, he was. Still there, standing stock-straight, gaze locked on her eyes, perhaps fighting whatever was pulling his attention to her bosom.

Another flutter of heat traveled through her.

He pointed at his door. "Rompole is with me. If Sancho needs to go out, just knock and one of us will see to him."

She reached for her belt and cinched it, and his gaze wandered all the way down to her bare toes and then skittered back up again, lighting an urge to throw herself at him. Thank heavens, he was chaperoned.

"I'm sorry I couldn't offer your man a room tonight. I don't know where Wes thinks he can put two footmen." She pointed down the corridor hoping for a respite from that molten gaze. "That door is a lumber room, and the other is Bixby's. We'll move Meg in with her and give Rompole Meg's attic room."

"There's no need. He's found a cot. Rompole and I have often shared quarters as needed." He smiled and another shiver went through her. "Sancho as well. If you wish to be rid of him, take him by the collar and bring him over to me."

He had Rompole, and she had Sancho, who would be a terrible chaperone. He'd probably welcome the Major into her bed.

And where had that thought come from? Perhaps she should move Bixby into her room to protect her from this madness. She might squeeze the maid in between her easel and the writing table.

He was looking at her again, and it made her flutter all over.

She never fluttered, except perhaps during those dinners under the relentless gaze of Sir Ebenezer. Steeling herself, she found her tongue and began babbling again.

"Yes, well, perhaps if the footmen are sturdy, they can shift things around and sleep in the lumber room. Bixby will not let them misbehave."

He stepped closer. "I *am* imposing, my lady."

5

A PERUSAL OF RUINS

So close, he was. Close enough for her to catch a whiff of the starch that stiffened his neck cloth, and the hint of brandy on his breath. A white hair stood out on his sleeve—a gift from Sancho—and her fingers itched to reach for him and brush it away. She gripped the ends of her belt and noticed the spot of dried lapis lazuli on the tip of one finger. "No." She shook her head. "Your bedchamber was completely available, as was Wes's. And my mother-in-law… well, I couldn't require her to climb an extra flight of stairs. I'd set this bedchamber aside as my, er, study, but my stay is intended to be so short, I never had the bed removed. So, you see, all is well."

His gaze slid over her shoulder into the well-lit room. "Is it also your studio?"

"I do paint in here."

He gave her a long look. "I hope you will one day let me see your work."

Her work. In her bedchamber. Oh, she might invite him in right now, but she wasn't the sort to welcome men into her bedchamber, in fact, she'd had a time of it keeping Melton's friends away.

And having him view her painting? He'd laugh, just like Melton and Wes always did.

His steady gaze had her hands itching again. She tugged her belt tighter, holding in the strange heat rippling through her. He wasn't so much interested in her amateurish rendering of York Minster as he was in her bosom because he couldn't seem to keep his gaze from moving there. She'd seen that sort of look before, though she'd never come close to this sort of inner turmoil before.

And blast it, this was her home. She wouldn't have male guests trying her on, be they distant cousins, or war heroes, or Sir Ebenezer look-alikes. Besides, she would have to face the morrow with him escorting her and Bixby.

"Well," she said, injecting a note of cheer. "I shall see you at breakfast and we may discuss what sights to see tomorrow. Do you have a particular interest?"

He bit his lip and smiled. "Yes, I find I do." He bowed. "Until morning then, my lady. Sweet dreams."

She closed the door and leaned her forehead against the cool wood. And then laughed. She'd been pursued before by the drunken sots Melton called friends. Jeremiah Ripton had been the most determined, but she'd always known she was no more than the fox or the hare they were chasing, and she'd never considered allowing herself to be caught.

Until now.

* * *

"IS ALL WELL?" GUS ASKED AS HE MET HONORIA IN THE front hall of her townhouse.

"I fear it is just the two of us today. Bixby feels it's imperative to stay here arranging Rompole's room and preparing for the arriving footmen. She has chores for your man as well."

"I see. Yes, put Rompole to work." Rompole didn't need his own room. In fact, the presence of a chaperone helped Gus curb his own baser urges toward the lady across the hall. But Gus sensed his servant might have an interest in the lady's maid, so he let the matter stand. "Did she wait until Wes departed to tell you this?"

Honoria gave an elegant little shrug that she might have learned in a French drawing room. He wanted to slip his arm over her shoulder and let his hand linger there.

"It's just as well," she said. "Bixby has no enthusiasm for historical sites."

"What does she like?" Rompole might like to know.

"She loves fashion, especially the French fashion plates. But only that. She's a country woman, and she has no interest in seeing Paris fashions on Parisians."

"Well at least she's not sporting a black eye." He raised an eyebrow. "Rompole asked your housekeeper about her injury."

She chuckled and led him out the front door. "Dunscombe attended a reform meeting last week. Matters got out of hand. She swears she didn't engage in fisticuffs but was injured making her escape."

"It's a very egalitarian household you run, my lady."

She halted and looked up at him. "As to that, Major, if we're to spend the day together, just the two of us, in an *indiscreet* perusal of ruins, you may as well call me Honoria."

"Is it still indiscreet if I'm along?"

She shrugged again, and he almost chucked her under her chin.

"Well then, you may call me Gus."

"On a day when I'm chasing Roman history, I rather prefer Augustus."

He bowed and offered his arm, and they proceeded down the street to the Shambles.

HOURS LATER, AFTER TOURING THE MINSTER WITH THE help of a guide, and resting a while on the benches inside, they proceeded to visit the city wall. As they turned a corner, the minster bells began pealing.

"Do you hear that?" Honoria paused in front of Bootham Bar and cocked her head. "Oh, they are glorious, are they not?"

She was glorious, but she wasn't ready to hear that from him yet. They'd ambled through the Shambles, where the lady ordered groceries and visited Orsini's apothecary, fetching powders for Cousin Genny. And then they'd visited the bookshops on Stonegate street and in Bookbinder's Alley, where he learned that, though she shared his interest in history, she also enjoyed the occasional romantic novel. He counted that as a good sign.

"They're certainly loud," Gus said. "But you're right, the sound is magnificent." He glanced at his fob watch. "It's an odd time for bells. In Spain, when the cannon balls weren't knocking over belltowers, the Papists rang the Angelus three times a day. Not at this hour, however."

"What adventures you've had. I suppose you've seen magnificent city walls like this one."

He gritted his teeth. He'd help knock a hole in a wall like this at Burgos.

The press of her hand on his arm brought him back to the present.

"Forgive me, Augustus. Your adventure wasn't a Grand Tour."

He set his hand atop hers. Watching her color rise did something to his heart and made him smile. "No forgiveness needed. Shall we walk on through the garden?"

"I'd rather walk along that wall and peer over it like a Roman soldier. Or…" she smiled up at him. Over the course of the morning, they'd settled into an easy companionship, and she'd beamed up at him like that frequently. "I know you will say the Romans didn't build those walls. But my guidebook says there were Roman-built walls there first. Probably not as sturdy as these."

"Oh, I don't know. The Romans built quite an ambitious wall to the north, and some of it stands today."

"Hadrian's Wall."

"Yes."

"I would *so* love to see that. The Romans had a fort at Brough, a short ride from Twisden Manor, but there is nothing Roman remaining, though there is a grand Norman-built castle on the site, or what remains of it. How I would love to explore something so ancient as Hadrian's Wall."

"Then you must come home with me to Whitlaw Grange and explore. I've discovered a little-known section of the wall running across my acreage."

"*Really?* How can you know?"

"I suppose I can't know for certain, oh ye of little faith. Perhaps it was part of a holding pen for the local cattle reivers. However, I've found a Roman coin or two in the area and, having visited a very sturdy portion of Hadrian's Wall north of Haltwhistle, I can say with some certainty that my stacked stones look just like theirs."

"And you found coins. I should *love* to see your bit of antiquity and sketch it."

"It's not as grand a subject as York Minster. Is that what you're painting?"

She'd brought out her pencil and a small pad during their tour of the Minster.

She nodded. "I have a very good view of it from my study."

"Your studio—bedchamber—study?"

She laughed and more color tinged her cheeks. "Yes."

He squeezed her hand. "Will you allow me to see it? The painting I mean. I draw a little, you know."

"As a gentleman ought to be able to do. I tried to tell Melton—my late husband—that Wes should have lessons. In fact, I enlisted one of his visitors to stay longer during one of Wes's school breaks and give both of us lessons. Melton said that was too much of a girlish thing." Her gaze shifted to the floor. "He said when our daughter was a little older, she and I could take lessons t-together." She eased in a breath and swallowed. "One miserably cold winter several years ago, before Melton deemed her old enough to paint, she was struck by a fever and… and I lost her."

An old grief swept over him. There was no greater pain for a parent, his mother said, after each of his siblings had died, and he knew that must be true, because he'd suffered as well. "She was your only child of the marriage?"

"The only one born to me. But of course, I have Wes."

She had Wes, and cared deeply for him, which explained why she tolerated so much from the lad.

"He's been mine since he was six, and I love him dearly. What of you, Major? You've told us much about your life, and yet so little. I might apply to my mother-in-law for more information, but I fear she doesn't know all your history. Did you ever marry?"

"No. And I have no children." As far as he knew. He'd always been careful. "I did, however, have a fiancée for all of two weeks, until some lordship's son and heir arrived at camp and the lady saw a chance for a coronet."

"Oh dear. You were crushed."

"As one is in those circumstances." The girl had done him a great favor, though, leaving him free to travel hither and yon in his soldiering, unattached and available for the lady before him. The thought of a future with her filled him with hope. "I did, however, recover."

"Aunt Honoria? Is that you?"

* * *

HONORIA TURNED AWAY FROM AUGUSTUS'S HEATED gaze and saw Patience advance with two of her stepdaughters—the twins. She groped for the names... Ivy and... Iris.

Glancing back, she saw a flare of interest in Augustus' eyes. Well, why not? Patience was young and beautiful, and so were the twins with their sparkling green eyes, auburn hair, and appealing sweetness.

Swallowing an unaccountable surge of envy, she hastened to make introductions—the girls had thankfully dressed in colors to match their names—

and watched as the twins latched onto each of the Major's arms, peppering him with questions about his army service.

Patience linked arms with her. "Look at those two magpies. I'm so happy I was able to give them a chance to put away their paints and have a Season."

"The girls paint?" There were so many Bigglesworth girls, she hadn't had a chance for a deeper acquaintance.

"Yes. Such lovely miniatures." She leaned in and whispered. "Their work is always in demand."

"I paint as well. A little. I should love to talk to them about their painting."

"You'll surely have a chance, though perhaps after we get through this ball. The plans are well underway, and the girls are busy sorting out gowns. We've sent the invitations and are starting to receive replies."

"I shall be there with Major Kellborn and my stepson, and they've both promised to dance with each of the girls."

Patience squeezed her hand. "Thank you, Aunt. I so wish my mother was alive to join us. She spoke fondly of you when I was growing up."

Honoria blinked back a surge of moisture. Her sister Emily had been shunned by the St. Aubyn's after her marriage to a man in trade. "Oh yes. Oh, how I missed her after she married. You must tell me all about—"

"*Mother. Gus. We've found you.*" Wes's voice boomed out, turning the feminine heads.

And Wes wasn't alone. Jeremiah Ripton had joined him in this ambush. The dastard was attired like a peacock from an earlier generation in a Pomona green coat and gold and red striped waistcoat.

6

A PICNIC AT KNAVESMIRE

*J*eremiah Ripton sent her an oily smile and bowed over each lady's hand as Honoria made introductions.

"What a jolly group of young ladies you must have," Wes told Patience. "Mother and I were planning to call on you tomorrow."

Patience smiled. "I shall make sure all the young ladies are there to meet you. Aunt Honoria tells me you've promised to dance with each of them."

"Indeed, I shall. As will my cousin here. Ripton, you must come as well and stand up with some of the ladies."

Patience sent Honoria an inquiring glance and said "Of course we will welcome another dancing gentleman. And now, we must run, as we are meeting Doro at one of the shops. Girls?"

"Must we?" Ivy said. "Oh, I suppose we must. But you must come along tomorrow, Major and answer all of our questions."

Iris giggled, and both girls went off with Patience.

"Handsome girls," Ripton said. "Lady Seahaven looks very young to have twins as old as Lady Ivy and Lady Iris."

"They're stepdaughters," Wes said. "Lady Seahaven's just a much younger stepmother than my dear mother here."

"The *ancient* one," Honoria murmured.

Wes nodded and went on, "And I daresay, Gus, Lady Ivy showed a marked interest in you."

She sighed. They were spirited and beautiful young ladies, and, for all that Augustus was much older, he was a fine-looking and virile man.

"They are merely curious girls," Augustus said, taking her hand and tucking it over his arm. "Wes, we ancient ones would like to continue our tour of York's ancient history. Shall we wish them good day, Honoria, and visit the ruins?"

Ripton laughed, too loudly. "We've been dismissed, sprout. Lady Twisden, I shall call on you tomorrow.

"No, that won't do," Wes cried. "Tomorrow we'll be out paying calls. You must come to dinner tomorrow night."

A shudder went through her. Ripton, at dinner—she'd hoped to never look across a table at him with a fork in her hand; the temptation to spear him might be too overpowering.

"We shall have Miss Jones even us up," she said.

Wes grimaced at that, as she knew he would, and Ripton smiled too broadly. "I should like to join you, but I have a previous engagement tomorrow night."

"The day after, then," Wes said. "What time, Mother?"

"The day after is Sunday," she said. "We'll have naught but a cold collation in the early afternoon, as the servants don't work on the Sabbath."

"Not one of them?" Wes frowned. "And I had no luck at the agency today. Well, you must come anyway, Ripton."

They sauntered off together, Wes wondering aloud about the nearest watering hole. Augustus watched them go, his thoughts indecipherable.

"Who is Miss Jones?" he asked. "Another candidate for the marriage mart?"

"Miss Jones? Hardly… but, oh, that is unkind. Why should she not seek marriage? Except, of course, that she's older than me, and I daresay older than you."

"I'm fast approaching the ancient age of forty," he said. "Eight-and-thirty to be precise."

"Ah, well, then I am just a green girl at three and thirty. But Miss Jones is perhaps of an age with Ripton. She's a gentlewoman fallen on hard times and my mother-in-law's companion. She didn't join us for dinner last night because she was moving my things and unpacking."

"A match for Ripton, then?"

Jones? The thought of the outspoken but dignified lady matched with Ripton made her shudder. "When Melton died, I persuaded Wes and his guardian to sell the hounds to Ripton. It was more important to repair the tenants' roofs than the kennel's dry rotted walls. Now *that*—a pack of prime hounds—was a good match for Ripton. I convinced Wes to keep back two bitches and a male and start his own pack." In the kennels, instead of the parlor, thank you very much. "Miss Jones tends to say what she thinks and offer unwelcome correction. Upon occasion to Wes."

He threw back his head and laughed. "Just what any young buck deserves. I look forward to meeting her."

The laugh changed him completely, driving out the dour, frightening warrior. She had a feeling he didn't laugh much, and she wanted to see him do it again.

TWO DAYS LATER

"You must come with us, Mother." Wes batted his hat against his leg. "Tell her Gus. It's a fine day, and Granny will like your company. The fresh air will drive away your headache."

Outside, Rompole was helping Cousin Genny and Miss Jones into the borrowed open barouche. With the three men accompanying them as outriders and Rompole playing coachman, there was plenty of room for Honoria and her maid. But of course, her maid had gone off to enjoy her free day, just like the other female servants.

Gus supposed that it was such a fine day that Honoria would rather work on her painting than journey out to Knavesmire to see the racetrack and grandstand. Plus, there was the matter of the unctuous Mr. Ripton, who'd taken a seat next to her at table that day, nudging her with his elbow. He'd continued to hover over her as she'd passed around cups of tea. It was especially annoying to hear him gush about what a particular friend Honoria was to him.

"I will stay here," Honoria said. "Enjoy your afternoon."

"I should like your company," Gus said, "but you need not come with us. You and Sancho must enjoy your peaceful afternoon. I'll scout for Roman ruins and drive you out to Knavesmire on another day."

"Let us at least bring Sir Sancho," Wes said.

She glanced back toward the dining room, where dishes still were still sitting out. Sancho would be needed here, and the loyal dog knew it.

"Come, Sir Sancho." Wes beckoned. Sancho remained seated and sent him a baleful look.

Gus clamped on his hat and took Wes by the shoulder. "Until later, Honoria."

Wes grumbled his way down the steps. "She'll go back and clear that table."

"Most likely."

"We could have had Rompole do it."

"He's playing coachman."

"There would have been a good chance for Ripton to walk with her and woo her."

The urge to smack the lad was overpowering. "On

that issue, she's made her feelings clear. If you open your eyes, you'll see it."

* * *

HONORIA TIDIED UP, LET SANCHO RUN WILD THROUGH the garden while she deadheaded flowers, and then went up to her studio.

She smiled. Her studio-bedchamber-study, as Augustus had called it. The smell of paint and turpentine greeted her. Sancho padded in behind her and sniffed.

"You did well today, Sir Sancho." The only rat that had caught his attention today was Ripton. He'd growled, actually growled, at the oily man. And then Sancho had intervened in almost every attempt by Ripton to sit close to her. She'd have given the dog a seat at the table if it wouldn't have been too shocking.

From across the table, Augustus had watched Ripton like Sir Ebenezer used to do in her fanciful imaginings at Twisden Manor. If Ripton had tried anything more than elbow-poking, Augustus might have drawn a fireplace poker.

She liked him. Well, perhaps more than liked him. He was intelligent and thoughtful, dignified, but no pompous ass. If she could believe her ears, they had a common interest in antiquities. Not art, perhaps; or at least not Turner's sort of painting. But at least he hadn't openly scoffed about Turner. She would have to broach the subject again and learn his true feelings.

And she would dearly love to hear about his travels—not the battles, not unless he wanted to talk about them.

He was just the sort of man she might once have dreamed of meeting, before she'd been shackled to Melton, before widowhood had granted her this liberty.

Sancho stopped at his water bowl and then scooted to his favorite spot under the bed clanking his collar along the floorboards, while she tossed aside her shawl, changed into an old gown and drew on her paint-stained smock. The complaint of a headache had not entirely been a lie, but bedrest wasn't called for. She needed to paint.

Drawing open the window, she let the spring breeze cool her cheeks while she studied the twin west towers with their gothic crowns and compared the image on her canvas. Close up, the detail was astounding; from a distance it was hard to render the magnificence. Was that line straight enough? Was the shading right?

She prepared her paints, one eye on the sky.

The view troubled her. It was true that the day was fine, but there was a miasma to the floating clouds, a yellowish-brownish haze that had nothing to do with sunlight filtering through. Coal smoke, perhaps? Though few people kept fires going once true winter had passed. She reached for her brush and palette and in a matter of minutes, lost herself in her work.

The sound of the kitchen door opening pulled her

out of her reverie. One of the servants was back early, and a good thing because she was parched. She'd ring for a cup of tea in a few moments.

Pausing to freshen her palette, she daubed on a bit too much tint. But never mind, she was no Turner after all.

Immersed in her murky sky, she didn't notice the minutes passing until the floor outside creaked and the door opened.

A low growl came from under the bed. Sancho had not entirely taken to Bixby, and he might not like the maid disturbing him, but at least Honoria would have her tea soon. "Shush Sancho," she said. "Greetings, Bixby. How was your afternoon?"

Sancho's nails tapped as he clattered out. She felt the swish of his tail and glanced down. He'd stationed himself before her, head lowered facing the door, growl deepening, poised to strike.

Air whooshed from her, and her breath tightened. This wasn't Bixby. Jeremiah Ripton had crossed her threshold.

She looked past him to the empty doorway and took in a slow breath.

"You've returned early," she said, keeping her voice steady. "Is Lady Twisden with you?"

"No, but I left her in good hands, probably enjoying her picnic by now. Kellborn went to fetch food from an inn." His gaze skittered to the floor. "Kindly call off his ill-trained cur."

"You mean to say, the others aren't with you?"

In reply, he smiled and licked his plump lips.

She heard her own breathlessness and tried to swallow the rising panic. Ripton had tried this sort of tactic before during a house party. Two of the hounds had saved her, and after that, during his visits, she'd slept in the nursery, or Bixby's room, or wherever he wouldn't find her. The man fancied himself handsome and irresistible. She'd never thought he'd follow her to York, or that Wes would be knuckleheaded enough to encourage it. Though, in fairness, her frankness with Wes hadn't stretched to bedroom matters.

She mustn't show fear or temper, which would only whet Ripton's desire. Yet, he would be made to leave, and soon. She'd find a way.

"With no horses running," she said blandly, "I knew Knavesmire would be a bore. Go down to the drawing room and wait for me. I'll come down directly as soon as I put away my paints and shed this smock."

His gaze trailed over the bulky smock. The stains were old; he might not recognize that most of the paint was dry.

His boot moved an inch and Sancho's growl erupted into a sharp bark.

She eased in a breath. "Come now, Ripton. You're an old friend of Sir Melton. Do take yourself downstairs and wait for me there. Wes will have some spirits somewhere, and I'll fetch them for you. Your presence here is inappropriate."

"Come now, Honoria."

The unctuous tone raised her hackles.

Unfortunately, he went on. "What could be more appropriate than Melton's old friend comforting his widow. You've allowed Kellborn to… why his bed is right across the corridor from yours."

"How would you know that unless… You've poked into the other bedchambers?"

"Looking for you, my dear. I wonder, hmm, have you discarded all that prim propriety, or was that all a ruse? If you're welcoming Kellborn to your bed, well, why not comfort an old friend who's just lost his wife?"

7

TO THE RESCUE

*B*ile rose in her. She quelled a momentary urge to spew out her luncheon and glared back at him. The answering heat in his eyes made her skin crawl, and she'd daresay, Sancho's as well. The dear boy was only a few vicious growls from clamping his jaws on Ripton's leg, and then who knew what retribution Ripton would attempt to wreak on the loyal dog?

Her fingers tightened around her palette and brush. She still had a thumb hooked in the hole in the palette and the fresh bubbles of color drew her attention.

For a man who'd just returned from a long ride to the country, Ripton was, aside from his boots, surprisingly dust free. His white neckcloth sparkled. His brown coat and blue and yellow brocaded waistcoat were unspotted. No mud colored his buckskins.

"This is outside of enough," she muttered. He'd

always been a peacock; let him look like one. She scooped a quick brushful of Rose Madder, added a generous bubble of Naples Yellow and held the brush before her like a wand. "Augustus Kellborn…" She jabbed at him and watched pigment fly… "is an officer and a gentleman. He would never enter my bedchamber…" She waved the brush and an orangey splat drove him a step back…. "Uninvited." With a quick flick of her wrist, speckles of paint stained his chin and neckcloth.

"Damn you, you vixen." He roared, snatched the brush, tossed it aside, and grabbed for her.

Before his pursed lips could clamp down on hers, he jumped back and roared again.

Sancho had a grip on the meaty buckskin. Ripton's hand flew out. The dog squealed, but the valiant lad had locked his jaws and didn't let go.

"How dare you." She slapped her palette against his face. Startled, he tugged at the board, but his hand slid away covered in paint and he looked at it in horror. She whipped the palette again and the business side struck the side of his head.

Genuine Ultramarine streaked from his temple down to his jaw, and a nicely blended orange dripped from his prominent nose. He looked so like an image she'd seen of an ancient Celtic warrior that she wanted to laugh, except that his burning eyes told her he'd be fetching his claymore soon.

"*It's your own fault,*" she shouted.

"You want to play?" he growled. "We'll play. First get this cur…" He shook his leg, trying to dislodge the dog, who was making his own attempt to shake the life out of Ripton's leg.

"I don't want to play. I want you out. Sancho, let him go."

Nothing happened.

"Sancho, suéltalo."

The commanding baritone came from the open door. Sancho froze, rolled his eyes that way, and let go of his prize with a deep growl.

"*Augustus.* Thank God you are here."

Ripton shook out his injured leg and glanced at the door. "Go away, Kellborn, and take your cur. Honoria asked me to find a way to return, and she and I are not finished." He brushed at his neckcloth, left a smear, and then, looking around, reached for her shawl.

"Stop right there." A fireplace poker came down on Ripton's arm with a sharp crack.

"Damn you," Ripton shouted.

Augustus had, in fact, armed himself with a poker. "Bless you, Augustus." She sent him a grateful smile and tossed Ripton her painting rag and watched him smear paint into his cheek.

Fresh paint stained her smock and her skirts; even Sir Sancho had not been spared. It was well worth it.

"Were you having a painting party, Lady Twisden?" There was humor in Augustus's voice.

"One must improvise," she said. "Creativity is at the heart of art."

Ripton wiped at his face, rubbing the paint around and removing very little of it. "Laugh if you will, Honoria. I can make things difficult for Wes. He thought to get those hounds back but—"

"Hounds? Wes doesn't want those hounds badly enough to…" She eased in a breath, steadying herself.

Dratted Wes. He probably did want the hounds, but surely he wouldn't have wanted *this*.

"I didn't want you in my bed at Twisden Manor and I don't want you in it here. And Wes? Why on earth would you threaten him? He's done nothing to harm you. In fact, he's made you the owner of the most prestigious kennel in all of Westmoreland. I wish you much joy of those hounds. Have them sleep in the bed with you every night. Melton did."

"As I recall they slept in your bed as well while you were visiting other bedchambers."

She grimaced, quelling the urge to slap him again. "You're absurd, Ripton. Augustus, if you'll show him out, I'll tend to Sir Sancho and then go back to my painting."

Augustus saluted and turned his icy gaze on her erstwhile ravisher. A shiver went through her along with a thrilling awareness as Ripton surrendered to a superior will.

When the door closed, she set aside her palette and brush, dropped to her knees, and pulled Sancho into a tight embrace, blinking back a rush of moisture.

"What a marvelous little warrior you are," she said, turning her cheek for his enthusiastic tongue.

With the skirt of her smock, she cleaned the worst of the paint from his sleek hair, examining him for injuries. "Cook's hambone will be yours, Sancho."

He licked away all her tears and left her laughing, and then took himself back under the bed.

Outside, the late afternoon sky was darkening, disrupting the view she'd been painting. The Minster was static, unmoving, a solid thing that had stood for centuries. But above, the clouds had shifted, like the state of her heart.

Her plans and her dreams weren't impossible. There might be idiots along the way, like Ripton, and annoyances like her meddling son, but a defender might come at just the right moment in the form of a valiant dog from under her bed or like a warrior stepping out of a centuries' old painting. She wasn't alone.

She glanced at her easel. Augustus hadn't had time to notice her painting. Thank goodness. The sky wasn't quite right. She found her palette and brush and went back to the canvas.

* * *

Gus said not a word as he escorted Ripton downstairs and opened the door, performing the duty with a decorum and civility the dastard didn't deserve.

Inside, he was seething. When he returned to the carriage with the basket of food from the inn and learned Ripton had left, he'd made his own excuses and departed, riding like the devil to get back in time. Honoria was alone in the house, and Ripton knew it.

For his part, Ripton, grumbled all the way down the stairs, cursing the paint that clung to his skin and clothing. He hadn't cursed Honoria yet. Just let him try.

Ripton paused at the door and glared. "I was provoked," he said. "Deceived. Honoria is—"

"A lady."

Ripton spluttered and then his gaze narrowed. "If you knew… why the hunting parties at Twisden Manor were absolute debauches."

"With the two Lady Twisdens in residence? I rather doubt that." He still gripped the fire poker he'd armed himself with. He might have to use it.

The fool went on, as if he hadn't spoken. "My wife wouldn't attend. But Honoria was there hosting all of them. And never in her bedchamber at night."

"But you were?"

Ripton blinked.

"In her bed?" Gus prodded.

Ripton's mouth firmed.

"Perhaps she was in her husband's bed," Gus said.

"Sir Melton? Hah. The man was impotent for the last ten years of his life. Blubbered about it to everyone when he was in his cups."

Gus sighed and opened the door wider. "On your way, sir, before Twisden and his grandmother return and start asking uncomfortable questions."

And before I have to beat you to a pulp.

The only horse on the street was his own. He

wondered where Ripton had left his. He hoped it was a long walk to a very public place so everyone could enjoy Honoria's brush technique.

Ripton took the few steps to the street, straightened his shoulders, and sneered back at him.

"And one more thing," Gus called before the other man could speak. "If I hear any more disparaging gossip, you and I will meet."

He closed the door and set the poker aside.

Honoria had been magnificent, wielding her paintbrush like a bayonet-tipped rifle, shooting splotches of color instead of lead. He needed to speak to her, privately, before the others arrived.

Upstairs, he paused at her door, wondering if she'd view his knock as another interruption worthy of more paint flinging. Chuckling, he decided he must take the risk to his neckcloth and coat.

8

A VIEWING AND A PROPOSAL

*B*efore he could knock the door opened.

"I wanted…" They both spoke at the same time.

He dipped his head and signaled that she should speak first.

"I wanted to thank you." She chewed on her lip and heaved in a breath. "And to disabuse you of the notion that I invited that… that imbecile to my bedchamber."

His opinion mattered to her. "Oh, my dear." Heart lifting, he started to reach for her and thought better of it. She'd just been assaulted by one suitor. Better to not rush his fences. "You're very welcome. And do not fear. I sized Ripton up the first night I met him." *And you.* "Only a loutish fool barges into a lady's bedchamber without permission."

"Quite." She paused, hands clutched at her waist. "And what was it you wanted?"

"I wanted to ask if I may enter and see your work."

Another long pause ensued. He held his breath, waiting.

"I see," she said finally. "Without barging in, you mean." Though no smile appeared, her lips quivered. "Will Sir Sancho bite you if you misbehave?"

"He won't because I won't misbehave. I find I very much value your good opinion and your friendship, Honoria."

"And thus, you will give me false compliments on my skills with the brush?"

"The brushwork I've observed so far today has been impressively creative."

She laughed then, a from-the-heart release of pent-up emotion, if he was any judge, and he couldn't help but join in.

"The blue on his cheek..." she said, choking. "Oh my. I suppose he'll go crying to Wes who thinks he's a capital fellow, but... Oh, Augustus, it's so nice to laugh with a friend."

"Then may I come in?'

Sancho poked his nose out, thumped his tale, and then slid back under the bed. Should Augustus turn out to be a lecher like Ripton, Sancho would be no help to her.

But... she didn't think he'd try to importune her, and even if he did...

She swallowed, remembering Sir Ebenezer's intense gaze from the canvas, so like Augustus's. Both men were so... dashing. To have all that heated warrior focus turned on her by a living man was almost irresistible.

If Augustus hated the painting, worse, if he made fun, would she be able to finish it? It was almost complete now, except for the sky. And of course, except for any touchups to the wobbly lines of the structure.

Who was she fooling? Even if he liked it, she'd go back and dab paint here or there until Midsummer arrived and her lease expired. Then she would have to stop, package it up and send it back to Twisden Manor for storage until she landed on her feet for good in some country cottage or city lodging. Perhaps by then there would be more paintings to share a wall with York Minster.

Augustus put up his hands. "Forgive me. I'll leave you in peace." He turned away.

"Wait." She reached for him, stopping just short of touching him with her paint-stained hands. Biting her lip, she nodded, and said "I was merely deciding. Please come in. If you hate it, you must feel free to tell me."

She could withstand the critique, somehow. *But please, God don't let him laugh at it.*

He went straight to the window first and looked out. The Minster rose behind the crowded buildings of the surrounding neighborhood, the twin towers touching the streaky sky.

"What a magnificent view," he said.

Then he stepped back and turned toward the easel. He paused for long moments, turning that intense gaze on her work. He didn't rub his chin, or shake his head, or nod. Only his eyes moved, up and down, side to side.

Then he looked at her and his lips turned up.

Her heart fell. He was going to make some joke about it as Melton or Wes would do. It was too blurry, the lines too indistinct, the colors all wrong.

"Yes," he said, nodding.

"Yes, what?"

He reached into his coat. "My sketchbook. I carry it with me often. An old habit from my Peninsular days when it was useful for, er, landscapes, and as a pastime to fill the quiet hours." He flipped open a page to a pencil sketch. "This is my work."

It was a picture of Sancho pouncing on prey. With just a few incisive strokes of the pencil the dog's vivacity leapt off the page.

"It's so very good, Augustus. His personality shines through. You must find my work dread—"

"No, that's not why I'm showing you this picture of Sancho."

At the mention of his name, Sancho crawled out from his under-the-bed lair.

"And here you are." Augustus's large hand settled atop the dog's head, his thumb sweeping over an ear.

Envy stirred in her. Or perhaps it was madness, to be envious of a dog.

As if he'd read her mind, he turned his smile on

her and went on. "When I viewed Turner's work in London, I didn't...well, I'm a literalist, I suppose. When one is outlining a plan of assault, precision is helpful. I've always been drawn to portraits, or paintings of horses." He laughed. "Or dogs. Yes, forgive me. I enjoy George Stubbs's work. And I like restful landscapes."

"Restful landscapes before battle."

He took her hand and his gaze slid to the canvas. "Yes. I've seen enough scarred, tumultuous landscapes after the fighting."

"Oh. Augustus, I'm sorry. It was thoughtless of me—"

"No." He set a finger to her lips. "What I'm trying to say is that Turner's work with his play on light and shade, and yours, are steeped in, well, *feelings*. Your Minster is marvelous, gothic, and haunting. Are you working on the sky?"

Marvelous. Did he truly mean that?

"The sky?" he prompted.

"The sky. Yes. One would like a beautiful blue, but this is closer to the true one as it is now."

"They say the strange skies and cold weather might be due to a volcanic eruption in Java two years ago."

"Yes," she said. "I read of that. It's such a big world." She would never see Java, but she'd like to go as far as France, and in her wildest dreams, Italy.

He nodded and pointed to the narrow settee at the foot of the bed. "May I sit while you work?"

The only person she'd ever allowed in the room

when she was painting was Bixby, who had no interest in art and who ignored her completely while she tended to Honoria's wardrobe.

"I won't comment or give advice," he said. "I have no skill with paints."

The mere notion of being watched made her hand tremble, but why not be brave? "Certainly. And here." She handed him back his sketchbook and pointed to the dog, who'd stretched out at her feet. "Sir Sancho is posing for you."

He smiled, drew out a pencil and opened to a blank page.

Nerves rattling, she picked up her palette, dipped her brush and turned back to the sky. A touch of yellow here. A hint of white there. Were her Minster towers too blurry? She stepped back and decided to leave them, and then returned to the sky until finally she had it right. Almost right. For now.

"We're losing the light." She tidied up and found her tinderbox, walking about the room and lighting lamps and candles while his pencil flew.

A thump and voices below stairs told her the others had returned.

"I suppose I must send you away before you're discovered here," she said.

He grunted, made one last flourish, and patted the empty space next to him. "Have a look. If you hate it, you must feel free to tell me."

She took off the smock and tossed it aside, deciding whether to take another risk. Like the bed, the settee could accommodate two people, but only if they squashed in close.

Heart racing, she squeezed in next to him, and accepted the sketch pad.

Her breath caught. The subject was a lady, shown in three-quarter view, her attention directed away, Tendrils of hair dangled at her neck and over her cheek. "It's meant to be me."

"Yes."

"She's too… That is how you see me? Well, the work is very precise, but to say that this is me…" She stood and he rose with her. "This lady is pretty."

"Yes. That is how I see you. You're pretty, Honoria." He tucked a lock of hair behind her ear and the heat rising in her cheeks rolled downward. "Shall I list your attributes? You have a straight little nose, full lips, hair the color of dark honey with the sun streaming through it, and rosy cheeks that seem to grow pinker when I'm around. A man notices a thing like that. And your eyes shine with intelligence and good humor. Yes. You are very pretty."

Speechless, she forced her mouth closed. Pinned under Augustus's dark gaze, she grew even warmer.

His big hand cradled her cheek, surprisingly gentle. "And I like your painting of the Minster. In fact, I should like to take it home with me to Whitlaw Grange and hang it over the mantel in my study. I should very much like to have you at Whitlaw Grange as well."

"My painting?" Over his mantel? She wasn't sure she wanted to part with it.

"Yes. And you must come as well. You can make sure it's correctly displayed."

"You want me to visit you? If you have ruins, perhaps I could paint... What? What are you doing?"

Augustus had dropped to one knee, sliding his hand down her arm to grasp her hand. Sancho bestirred himself and stretched.

"I don't want you to come for a visit, Honoria. I want you to come as my bride. Will you marry me? Will you make me the happiest of men?"

Marry? Marry Augustus Kellborn?

His dark gaze pulled at her like a magnet, the desire in his eyes matching the heat rising in her. Her head dipped. Just a few inches more and...

She straightened and tried to get hold of herself. "We've had but one outing together."

"And one dinner and luncheon. And don't forget we attended church together."

"You rescued me, and now you are being chivalrous. You're acting in haste, and there is no need."

His eyes twinkled. "I'm chivalrous? I rather like that."

"You're smiling now. That is better. Now, please, get up."

He complied, still holding her hand. "You haven't answered my question, Honoria. Will you marry me?"

Heart hammering, she stared up into his dark, intent gaze. "Augustus, you must agree this is precipitate. You cannot mean… you'll meet a bevy of young women looking to marry."

"It's you I want."

"But… but." He'd shown no interest beyond what was polite and appropriate for a house guest. "Until now, I had no notion… no hint of any interest on your part."

"I escorted you on your outing. I sat next to you at church. I would have snared your hand for a private stroll away from the picnickers today if you'd gone along with us. When I saw that Ripton had disappeared, I had a suspicion he'd be coming back here, so I returned in all haste only to find you rescuing yourself. And now, I want to make my intentions clear."

"Clear?"

He nodded. "Yes."

Did he feel the same wicked heat rising as she did? There was humor in his dark eyes, not lust.

She shook her head. "I don't think you can be serious, Major Kellborn. Offering marriage when you haven't so much as tried to kiss—"

"Kiss you? Why so I haven't." He leaned close and brought his lips a hair's breadth from hers. "May I, my lady?"

Her heart threatened to melt into a puddle. He was letting her decide.

A spurt of madness lifted her heels, tipping her forward.

Her lips touched his in a featherlight connection. He angled his head and brushed a kiss over the corner of her mouth, over her cheek, and jaw, and down to her neck where his touch sent a ripple of need through her. Such softness, such tenderness, from such a hard man—it was a marvel, one that sent her hand sliding around his waist, and her other groping for his shoulder. She raked through the dark curls of hair at his collar and when he brought his lips back to hers, sighed and gave herself up entirely.

While he was gentle, she grew demanding, and he accommodated her, touching her, letting her sighs and moans guide his skilled fingers. In the dark recesses of her mind, the thought flashed that Melton had never kissed her like this.

She ran a hand down his chest and while his lips found the spot on her neck again, she glanced at the bed.

Augustus lifted his head and stepped back, his hands at her shoulders steadying her. A moment later the door opened.

She heard a startled gasp, and then the sound of the door snicking shut.

Heat burning her cheeks, she laughed. She was a wanton who'd just been eying up the bed and plotting to lead Augustus there. Who would have known? She'd certainly shocked Bixby—that had been her maid's wheezy gasp.

When she lifted her chin, she found Augustus watching her. The look was… almost smug, and that thought made her smile again. He had a right to his little victory. If he was aiming at seduction, he didn't require much more persuasion than that kiss, which was so much more than any kiss she'd ever shared with her husband or had stolen from her by one of his brash drunken friends.

She was a widow. She could do what she'd never done as a married lady—she could take a lover, one who was, if she wasn't mistaken, highly skilled. Well, at least more skilled than Melton, because how would she know beyond that?

"I am very glad you asked for that kiss," he said. "I am certain now that we will suit."

She had asked for the kiss? Well, she supposed she had. It didn't mean she would marry him. They would suit in that way for a while, but she knew they would eventually have to leave the bedchamber and then what? Then she'd find herself in a moldering manor house far on the outside of nowhere, running a household while he hunted and fished and went to horse auctions with her stepson. She'd have little time to search out Roman ruins, and she'd never visit Paris, or any other grand foreign city.

She wanted to see something of the world before she retired to kick up her feet in the country. Augustus would want to marry and be home by Michaelmas. And he'd want to start filling his nursery.

At the thought of babies, her throat thickened with longing. She'd loved and lost her child, and there'd been no others. Many children didn't survive, so the more babies a man fathered, the greater his chance for an heir. Augustus needed a young wife for that, not a widow of three and thirty.

She wouldn't marry him, but perhaps she could pay him a visit, as soon even as next summer. After all, she *would* like to see those Roman ruins on his estate. Perhaps there'd be a christening, and all of his new-found Twisden relations could attend.

And for that reason, she wouldn't take him as a lover. Imagine greeting his young wife a year from now, especially if he married one of Patience's girls? She was, perhaps, putting too fine a point on it, but making love to Augustus would feel like betraying his future wife.

9

ROMPOLE'S ASSIGNMENT

*H*onoria's body was saying yes, but Gus could see that her mind was working through a series of arguments about his proposal, and taking her to a decided no.

Well at least she knew where he stood; and he knew she wanted him. And he certainly wanted her. More negotiations would have to follow. More wooing. How he was supposed to go about that, he wasn't sure.

He'd complimented her painting—sincerely, as it turned out. And he'd kissed her, and she'd kissed him back quite ardently, instead of slapping him with her paint brush.

He still had a chance with her, he just needed to puzzle out the right tactic.

"We've shocked your maid," he said. "I take it she's never seen you in the arms of a man other than your husband?"

"She's never seen me in any man's arms." She

shook her head. "That kiss was… a revelation. But I must say—"

He set his finger to her lips. "Say nothing." A revelation, was it? Well, then, he definitely had a chance. He just needed to forestall any more buts and learn what else she was looking for in a husband. "My offer stands on firmer ground than ever." If only she knew how firm he was feeling. "But be assured, I won't invade your bedchamber. I'll wait for an invitation."

He tucked an escaping curl behind the feminine shell of her ear, dropped a kiss on her forehead and crossed the hall to his own room.

Rompole was there applying a shoe brush to a boot with some violence. "Annoying woman," he said.

"I beg your pardon?"

"Not Lady Twisden." Rompole looked away, biting back a smile. "I mean her scrawny maid, Bixby."

"And when did you encounter her? She wasn't along for the picnic. Where are the others?"

"Which question do ye want me to answer first?" Rompole raised an eyebrow, and when Gus crossed his arms, he laughed. "The young sir spotted a gaggle of red-haired young ladies he knew and had me haul all of them to a fine house and return the carriage. I ran into *that woman* on the street, and she buttonholed me again with questions, fretting and complaining all the way home."

"Again?"

"Aye. Pain in my arse, she's been."

Gus shrugged out of his coat. "What is Lady Twisden's maid asking about?"

"France. Her lady is fixing to travel there come July and is taking her along. She don't want to go. Don't want to get on a packet boat. Don't want to deal with foreigners especially since she don't speak the language and her lady only knows a smattering."

He crossed to the small chest of drawers where a bottle of brandy stood three-quarters full and poured himself a dram.

Honoria had plans. What an idiot he was. He hadn't thought ahead to what she would do after York. He'd supposed she'd return to Twisden Manor—in fact, Wes had implied that she'd return there, at least when he wasn't plotting her marriage to Ripton. And he himself, being another male dunderhead, though not so great a one as Wes, had fixed on preventing the abomination of a marriage to Ripton and never questioned the notion of Honoria returning to Twisden Manor.

"Where in France are they going?"

"Bixby ain't going there. Looking for another position and wringing her hands over it. Can't be responsible for her lady when it's just two ladies traveling alone, an' she's not to tell the young sir else he'll hop on the boat and go with them. She had a mind to do just that, 'ceptin' then they'd have him along and he's a thorn in her side and everyone else's."

Wes would want to follow Honoria to France just

like he'd followed her to York. Perhaps he'd think to bring Ripton along as well for the trip.

But two women alone traveling through France—Bixby was right. Honoria was smart, and solid, but not sophisticated. And if she didn't have friends there to guide her...

Rompole frowned and shook his head. "Can't say as I disagree with her about the lad."

He raised an eyebrow at his valet. Further chastisement wasn't needed because he couldn't disagree either. Wes was young, and lively. Gus had enjoyed Wes's company in Brampton and at Twisden Manor, and, finding himself a bit bored at the time, had jumped at the offer of hospitality in York. Where Wes's mother—stepmother actually—was concerned, the *young sir*'s exuberance led to a tendency to be overbearing.

The lady wanted to travel. He'd like to see France again himself, and not with a saber in hand. It would make for a lovely honeymoon destination. Bixby could travel on to Whitlaw Grange, if she wanted to stay in her lady's employ, and they'd hire a temporary French maid for the new Mrs. Kellborn.

Would she trust him? Would she believe his good intentions? Would she say yes?

He needed to know exactly where she wanted to go.

"Rompole," he said. "I have an assignment for you."

* * *

"You take up too much room." Honoria nudged the backside wedged up next to her in the bed. When her bedmate lifted his head and yawned, she pulled her hand from under the covers and ruffled his ears.

In the days since his master's marriage proposal, Sir Sancho had moved from his safe hidy-hole under the bed to the soft coverlet on top. He'd performed his extermination duties admirably; it had been days since he'd dropped a prize at her feet, so she'd allowed him the comfortable respite.

Since her elder sister, Emily went off to be married, Honoria had always slept alone, even during her marriage. When Sir Melton's hounds found their way into her bedchamber instead of his, she swiftly chucked them out. Surprisingly, she didn't mind the little terrier's presence. In fact, even in this smallish bed, he took up little room. Besides, he was always a gentleman, rather like his master.

Reminded of the master in question, she reached for the book on the bedside table. Morning had broken with enough light for her to peruse *Galignani's Paris Guide*. It was the last in a series of travel guides delivered from the shop in Bookbinder's Alley, all for Augustus. Gargiolli's guide to Florence had been the first, followed by Nibby's Roman guidebook, and Miss Starke's highly detailed travel memoirs, *Adapted for the Use of Travelers and Including a Guide to Sicily*.

Sicily! Having read the historical account included, she'd added the island as a desired destination.

She'd intercepted the books and burnt her candles to nubs reading them before having Meg deliver them to Augustus's room. Odd that, despite spending almost every day in his company, he hadn't mentioned a desire to travel. And she didn't bring it up. They'd attended a party, a picnic, a musical night, and visited a gallery, always in company, never alone.

What was he up to? Perhaps she should just walk across the hall and knock on his bedchamber door, hand him the book and ask.

No doubt though, it would be Rompole answering. Augustus would be out on an early morning ride.

She pushed back the covers and stood. Patience's ball was tonight, and it seemed possible that there would be a betrothal announced—perhaps more than one. She'd promised to pay a call on her niece and help with last minute preparations, but nevertheless, she must find a moment in this busy day to speak with Augustus.

Chuckling, she shrugged into her robe and went to the washstand. Perhaps she'd confess that she'd waylaid his books, and he could help her plan her itinerary. In fact, she'd bring the Paris guide to the breakfast table, and give it to him in person.

* * *

GUS WAS THE FIRST TO ARRIVE AT THE BREAKFAST table.

The surly housekeeper entered after him with the

coffee urn, a plate of toast, and a question about his eggs.

He was comfortable with her directness; she reminded him of Rompole. His own housekeeper was just as efficient, but far more deferential. In the many long months since he took up residence at Whitlaw Grange, he'd kept a close eye on the servants, and gone over all the estate books himself. His housekeeper, his butler, and his steward, all local people, happy for the work, ran a tight and honest ship. He was content to leave them to it.

He hadn't realized how much wanderlust he was feeling until Wes invited him to visit York. And if Honoria wanted to travel to the Continent—well, he'd be happy to show her every old church between Calais and Palermo.

"What, ho? Up already? And you went riding. Why didn't you wake me?"

Wes had arrived.

Gus slid the plate of toast his way, wished him good morning, and teased him about sleeping late.

"You'll wish you slept in when you're yawning through the steps of a quadrille, Gus. And don't forget, you've promised to dance with all the young ladies. Isn't that right, Mother?"

Honoria stood in the doorway carrying a book. When he smiled at her, her color rose in that enticing way he wanted to explore more.

Gus pulled out the chair next to his and waved her over. "You promised me two dances, Honoria, my love. They must be waltzes."

"I say." Wes looked up from his cup. "Are you flirting with my stepmama, Gus?"

The young buck had finally noticed.

"What have you there?" Gus ignored him and nodded at the book.

"This was delivered for you yesterday, Augustus."

"A book?" Wes asked. "What book?"

Gus reached for the tome, sliding his hand around her much smaller one, feeling the jump in her pulse. "It's the latest travel guide to Paris, Wes. Did you have a chance to look at it, Honoria?"

She smiled, and then laughed and took her seat. "I couldn't help myself. It's so filled with fascinating details."

"You must feel free to borrow it. I have others for Florence, Rome, and Sicily. Those are at your disposal as well."

Wes's knife paused above the marmalade dish, and he looked up. "You're making a Grand Tour, Gus? Why, what with the war, I never had one myself. Father always talked about what fun he had on his. When are you leaving? After the races, surely. We'll dash home then, and I'll prepare to go with you. Mother, you can keep Twisden Manor in hand while I'm gone, can't you?" He gazed toward the window. "Paris," he said, dreamily.

Honoria's gaze had dropped to her empty plate. Gus reached for her hand and squeezed it.

"Actually," he said, "I've lost interest in the races. And, much as I enjoy your company, Wes, I have a different traveling companion in mind for a visit to Paris."

She turned an astonished gaze on him, her face flooding with delicious color.

"Yes." He smiled. "Paris. Then Lucerne, Venice, Florence, and the ruins in Rome. A packet to Sicily. Then, perhaps a stop in Malta. I have a friend there who would welcome our visit."

"See here." Wes had stood. "What—"

"Oh, sit down, Westcott," Honoria said.

He felt her small hand rotate within his and squeeze him back.

"I'm not returning to run Twisden Manor," she said. "That is *your* responsibility, and if you need a hostess, your grandmama will relish the duty until you find your own Lady Twisden."

Wes remained standing, his color rising, his glower deepening.

"My intentions are entirely honorable," Gus said.

"Are they? And you, Stepmama. Father's been dead little more than a year."

"Yet you were anxious to hand me over to Ripton," Honoria said calmly. "Who, by the way, Wes, is most assuredly not interested in marriage."

The red flames in his cheeks deepened to purple.

"You didn't know," Honoria said. "But of course. You thought he was a gentleman like your father, or you."

"I'll speak with him," Wes spluttered. "With father dead, I'm the head of this family and—"

"Don't be a goose," Honoria said. "He's no

different than many of your father's other friends. Probably like many of the young gentlemen you know. And he's your near neighbor. You'll want to keep on good terms with him."

"He's different than *me*," Gus said. "I repeat, my intentions are entirely honorable."

Whatever thoughts flew through Wes's young brain contorted his lips and brows until he finally resumed his frown. "You must speak to me first, Gus."

"Westcott," Honoria said. "You are the child of my heart. I love you, and I would never shame you, and though you are the head of the family now, this house in York is mine until Midsummer. Mrs. Dunscombe," she signaled the housekeeper who was lurking, eyes bright with interest. "Sir Westcott will take his breakfast in the drawing room. Please see that he's comfortable there."

"*Mother!*"

"Augustus and I need a private moment. Close the door on your way out, Wes."

"You may issue your challenge later," Gus said, unable to resist the urge to tease the lad.

"There'll be no need for that," she said. "We will come in and speak with you in a moment."

* * *

WHEN THE DOOR CLOSED, AUGUSTUS TOOK HER OTHER hand in his, sending her heart pounding, as if it wasn't already slamming her ribs like a blacksmith's hammer.

"Which of the guidebooks was your favorite, Honoria?"

She let out a breath. "You knew? How—"

"Bixby told Rompole."

That news wasn't surprising. Her maid had been fretting since they left Westmoreland. She was a countrywoman with no spirit of adventure. "The traitor."

"She fell into my plan readily. According to Rompole, she really doesn't want to travel."

His thumb swept over the back of her hand, and her breath tightened around the familiar scent of shaving soap, and leather, and horse, addling her brain further.

"We may have just met," he said, "but I've known of you through my mother's letters. *How lucky Twisden is*, she used to say. *He's found such a clever and good lady.* She wanted me to find someone like you to take as my bride. And then, when I met Wes, he said the same thing, that you were *clever and good*."

"And old," she whispered.

Gus threw back his head and laughed. "You can imagine my surprise when his stepmama turned out to be a pretty young widow not at all in her dotage. I wanted to yank him up by his neckcloth and shake him."

"I should like to have seen that. Though... he is rather taller than you."

"But not as experienced with yanking neckcloths."

"Very true." Wes was a pudding head sometimes. Taking up his father's baronetcy had puffed him up too much. "Imagine him trying to fight a duel with you Augustus. I worry about him."

"He'll be all right, Honoria. I don't think he'd ask to meet over just any small slight. He adores you, you know."

Tears sprang to her eyes, and she squeezed them back.

"I've a great deal of experience I could apply to advising Wes as his stepfather."

Moisture flooded her throat and she couldn't speak.

"That is, advising by letter. Otherwise, in-person talks will come after the honeymoon. And only when we are in the neighborhood of Westmoreland and not traveling."

He had more traveling in mind than the Grand Tour he'd outlined today? "But what about your estate?"

"We'll spend time there, as well. You must paint those ruins for me. After our honeymoon."

Dizziness threatened, and the squeeze of his hands steadied her.

"I have good people in place at Whitlaw Grange, and I'll take you there first when we return. Perhaps by next spring or next summer. We'll invite the rest of my newly discovered Twisden relations."

Hadn't she thought of visiting for a christening then? A child to hold and to love. It wasn't impossible.

She blinked back tears and shook off the thrill of that hope. "I thought that you had an interest in Ivy or Iris. A younger woman would—"

"No," he said. "Never. It's been only you, Honoria, from the moment I crossed your threshold. This inheritance was a surprise from a childless relation on my mother's side. If you and I don't have a child, I suppose we shall just have to leave Whitlaw Grange to Wes."

His dark eyes glowed with intensity, reminding her of Sir Ebenezer, who'd simultaneously frightened and intrigued her. Augustus didn't frighten her.

What sort of man was he? He'd served the Crown honorably for decades. He'd been a good son to the mother who'd shared stories in letters to Wes's grandmother. He'd been patient with Wes. He had a regard for family. He wasn't a weasel like Ripton, or an oaf like Sir Melton.

And he hadn't laughed at her painting.

And his kiss…

She freed her hands and tugged him close. "When do you plan for this journey to begin?"

He reached under his coats and produced two documents. "This," he said, "is a letter from an agent in London."

She perused the lines. He'd booked passage three weeks hence to Calais on the King George for himself and his wife.

Three weeks. She couldn't become his lady in three weeks' time. They'd first need to call the banns and then marry, and then still have time to travel to catch the packet…

She was falling into his plan just as Bixby had.

A firm finger lifted her chin. "Honoria, my love, I have more than ample funds to pay for the trip. This other document is a license from the bishop here. We have five days to fashion a proper settlement—you may keep all your dower, and I will provide for our children out of my funds—and then we'll be married at the Minster."

"You obtained a license. That was very… very confident of you."

"Yes. What say you? Will you be my bride?"

She glanced at the agent's letter again. Travel to France. As the bride of this man… who she wanted.

She wouldn't go as his mistress. She'd meant what she said about not disgracing Wes. And he meant what he said about his honorable intentions.

And… children. He was thinking of that too, and why not? She wasn't too old for children.

When his fingers brushed her cheek, she had a good look into his eyes and saw a hint of uncertainty, a touch of vulnerability, a dogged determination. And admiration. For her, a plain widow of three-and-thirty.

Their lips met, drawn together by matching desire, and need, and true regard. Hearts pounding in time, their tongues dueled and long moments later Honoria found herself on his lap, her hair spilling around her shoulders.

And then suddenly, he'd set her back, one hand

cupping her breast, the other her cheek. "An answer, my lady."

"Yes," she said. "Yes, yes, yes."

* * *

IT WAS SIR SANCHO WHO FINALLY INTERRUPTED THEM. Gus heard the door to the breakfast room open and paused with his hand down the front of Honoria's gown. He saw a flash of white fur and heard the dog scamper past and went back to his ministrations.

Moments later, Sancho pounced on Gus's boots.

"Stop it," Gus said. "You're scratching the leather. Rompole will skin you alive."

With a defiant bark, Sancho pounced again.

Honoria drew in a sharp breath and he followed the line of her gaze.

A dead mouse lay at their feet—a gift from Sir Sancho. She squirmed, breathlessly sucking air and then jumped off his lap and pointed.

On the table, a mouse munched on the corner of toast he'd abandoned for sweeter things.

"To arms," he said, and tossed the terrier onto the table.

Her hands flew first to her cheeks, and then over her eyes. "Not on my breakfast table," she wheezed.

Locks of hair fell over her cheeks and shoulders. She looked ridiculously tumbled and lovely, her lips pink and puffy, her bodice loose.

In moments, Sancho had conquered, and by the time Honoria opened her eyes he'd arrived at her feet with his offering, leaving a battlefield of splashed coffee, toppled salt cellars, and forks strewn about like the sabers of the fallen.

Her eyes squinted hotly. "Sir Melton's hounds—"

"Were ill-behaved. I know. Wes told me." He'd been just as appalled at the stories as Honoria.

"I won't have—"

"No, Honoria. I wouldn't have had to send him into the fray if we'd been paying attention. It was our fault, you see. In the future, we must pay better heed. And your rules, my love, will apply. We'll even prevent him from sleeping under our bed if that is your wish."

A fresh wash of color rose in her cheeks.

"Or on our bed." He laughed. "Yes. I heard he'd weaseled his way into a more comfortable spot. Bixby told Rompole." He went to the door and found, as he suspected, both her maid and his valet lurking. He beckoned them in, crossed the room and took Honoria in his arms.

"Rompole, Bixby, you may be the first to wish us happy. And then, Rompole, dispose of these bodies. Bixby, your mistress needs your assistance." He dropped a kiss on her forehead. "Honoria, my love, I'll just go speak with the *head* of the family. Why don't you join us in a few minutes?"

She smiled, and then laughed. "Oh, I will. Melton wasn't much of a disciplinarian with the lad. Don't thrash him too badly when you take him in hand."

.

EPILOGUE

LATE JULY, 1817

RUE DE LA PAIX, PARIS

*H*onoria's brush paused over her palette, and she studied the small canvas before her. The painting was, perhaps, finished.

"Lovely." Strong arms came around her waist causing her hand—and in truth, her insides—to tremble. Not her stomach though. That had finally settled for this day.

"I thank you for waiting until I lifted the brush." She'd sensed more than heard her husband's stealthy approach, detecting a waft of his citrusy shaving soap and the currents of air in the still room.

"Yes, I remembered to be cautious of your brushwork," he murmured.

She leaned back and savored his embrace. "What think you, Augustus? Shall I add more color? The sky is rather bluer today. Perhaps less yellow, more blue?"

Fingers brushed at her hair. A kiss to her neck stirred a shiver.

"It's whatever you see, my love. You're the artist."

"I don't want future visitors of Whitlaw Grange to comment that all of my skies were murky-muddled."

"Mmm-hmmm." He pushed the neckline of her robe away and uncovered the strap of her nightgown. "I'm glad you're feeling better this morning."

She squashed a laugh. Almost three months married, and Augustus's interest hadn't waned. Nor her own. In fact, she'd discovered an untapped enthusiasm for marital relations.

Because of Augustus, because of his regard, and caring, and love.

As it turned out, they'd stayed for the York races, returning from a brief honeymoon—and privacy—in Harrogate to the house on St. Hedwig's Place. They'd attended the Antiquarian Society lectures and been witness to more than one happy engagement. Honoria wasn't the only one well settled. Patience's girls had done well during their Season in York. And Patience herself… well, her dear sister's daughter had found her own second chance at happiness.

Unencumbered by their servants and dog—Rompole, Bixby, and Sir Sancho had retired to Whitlaw Grange—Honoria and Augustus had made a leisurely trip first to London and then on to France. In Paris, they'd spent mornings in bed, afternoons touring, and evenings strolling along the Seine. Here and there, she'd sketched, and finally settled on the simplest view —from this window of their hotel bedchamber where the Palais Brongniart, the Paris stock exchange stood. Though the building was still under construction, her painting was complete. Probably.

"What think you, Honey? If you are finished with Paris, shall we move on. Where would you like to go next?"

She laughed, quickly set aside the brush and palette, and turned into her husband's arms. "You decide."

He cradled her jaw in his hand. "Chartres, I think," he said. "But first…"

He slipped a hand under her knees, and she found herself floating, and laughing, and landing softly atop the big bed.

Opening her arms, she welcomed him, and brushed back a lock of dark hair from his eyes. "I see you are letting your hair grow," she teased. "Very soon you'll look even more like Sir Ebenezer."

His lips quirked. "My ancestor? The fellow whose portrait hangs in Twisden's dining room?"

"Yes." She'd never told Augustus about her Sir Ebenezer imaginings. But that could wait. She had other news to share. "I think we ought to ask Wes for that painting, or at least have it copied."

"What is that dreamy-eyed look, wife? I'm feeling a prick of jealousy." His smile, and the light touch of his finger tracing her jaw told her he was teasing her back.

"Sir Ebenezer used to keep watch during Sir Melton's dinner parties. It was a great comfort to me, having a fierce warrior staring daggers at some of the guests."

"You have me for that task now."

"Too true, and I absolutely love you for it. But I was thinking, we might hang your portrait next to Sir Ebenezer's. And then, on cold winter's nights, we can tell the children the story of their ancestor's battles with reivers."

He lifted his head, and then propped himself up on an elbow, his gaze searching her face, a smile slowly breaking. "It wasn't the escargot making you queasy."

She tapped his nose. "I wondered how long it would take you to notice. And it's far too early to be sure of anything." She raised her head for a quick kiss. "Is your heart set on Rome? I'm willing to forgo the Colosseum and travel straight to Sicily."

"The Romans were there as well. But can you—"

"Yes. There are excellent midwives in France. I shall consult with one and then we may set out. I'll sketch but leave off painting at each stop. We'll take our time, and even traveling by easy stages, we can be home by Christmas."

"You've thought this through." He frowned and opened his mouth, and she set his finger to his lips before he could speak.

"No one can predict the future, Augustus. Tell me,

were there not women with child following the drum? I know that I'll have an easier time than they did."

"Very well. But we must keep you well fed, and well rested, and, as you said, travel by easy stages." He fell back and stared up at the canopy. "And perhaps I'd better not make demands—"

"Oh no you don't." She rolled atop him, nipped at his neck, heard his soft chuckle, and felt his surrender.

The End

A NOTE FROM THE AUTHOR

I hope you've enjoyed reading Honoria's and Gus's story, which I wrote during a time when my husband was very ill, shortly before he passed away.

Many thanks go to my writer friends at the Bluestocking Belles, Caroline Warfield, Jude Knight, Sherry Ewing, Rue Allyn, Elizabeth Ellen Carter, and Cerise Deland for their encouragement and support during that terrible time and for their help with this story. Thanks go also to Dar Albert of Wicked Smart Designs for the beautiful cover.

I do believe Honoria's stepson, Wes, needs to be brought to heel, and I hope to get to his story someday.

To find out more about my books, visit my website, https://alinakfield.com, and sign up for my monthly newsletter.

All the best,

Alina K. Field

ALSO BY ALINA K. FIELD

Sons of the Spy Lord Series

Marrying Mr. Gibson

Previously titled *The Bastard's Iberian Bride*

Paulette Heardwyn rushes to visit her dying guardian, set on learning the truth about her father. But the only man with answers takes his secrets to the grave, leaving her penniless—unless she marries his illegitimate son

The Viscount's Seduction

Lady Sirena Hollister has lost everything, even her fey abilities. But when the fairies hand her a chance at a London Season, her schemes for revenge stir up an unknown enemy, and spark danger of a different sort, in the person of a handsome Viscount.

The Rogue's Last Scandal

Falling—literally—into the arms of the *ton*'s most outrageous rogue seems a risky path of escape, but Maria Graciela Kingsley y Romero has no other choice. Only England's greatest spy lord can help her, and he is not to be found—so his son will have to do!

The Counterfeit Lady

Vowing she'll never submit to an arranged marriage, an earl's daughter bolts for the seaside cottage that will someday be hers. But she finds her quiet refuge occupied by the last man she ever wants to see—an American artist, who's also a thief. And, quite possibly one of her father's spies.

Avenging the Earl's Lady

The long war is over, but honor requires vanquishing one last enemy, and the Earl of Shaldon has no time for romance. But when the lady he longs for interferes in his plot, and his enemy strikes at her, nothing else matters but avenging his lady.

Novellas and Holiday Stories

The Marquess and the Midwife

A Christmas Novella

Finalist, 2016 National Reader's Choice Award

Uncovering a lie drives a new marquess back from a self-imposed exile at Christmas to find the only woman he's ever loved. Finding her turns out to be easy, uncovering her stunning secrets, a bit harder. But winning her back will be the greatest challenge of all.

A Leap Into Love

A Sweet Regence Romance Novella, a sequel to

The Marquess and the Midwife

Can a gentleman be too charming?

The ladies of Upper Upton think so.

When the single ladies of the village conspire to teach their charmer a lesson that might bankrupt him, the town's loveliest young widow—who's sworn off marriage forever —steps up to warn him.

Liliana's Letter

Finalist, 2015 National Reader's Choice Award

The Matchmaker Meets the Matchbreaker

Liliana Ashford's future as a professional chaperone depends on her wealthy charge's successful marriage, but her own close encounter with a scoundrel years ago makes her determined to save the girl from the same kind of rogue.

The Ghost of Depford Hall

A short, sweet Halloween story, a sequel to

Liliana's Letter

It's her mother's last All Hallows' Eve.

When family, friends, and tenants gather, goblins, ghouls, and ghosts are banned from this All Hallows' Eve party.

Only, no one told the Ghost of Depford Hall!

Courted by the Earl

Previously titled *Bella's Band*

A 2015 RONE Award Finalist

Saddled with his brother's title and debts, nothing about this new life makes the Earl of Hackwell want to stay—until he meets a lady with a secret that can change everything.

Rosalyn's Ring

2014 Book Buyer's Best Winner, Novella Category

Done with grieving her losses, a late nobleman's daughter has fallen into a tidy spinster's life in London. But when one snowy Christmas Eve, a young woman needs rescue, she seizes the chance to do good—and to recover a family heirloom that ought to be hers.

Haunting Miss Fenwick

Thrilled to finally have a permanent home, a Squire's daughter won't let a supernatural creature scare her away. While hunting the ghost she doesn't believe in, she stumbles upon a mysterious flesh and blood man who might be the key to all of her problems.

The Upstart Christmas Brides Series

The Duke She Despised

Hiding her true identity, a young vicar's widow takes a position as housekeeper in a remote Scottish castle at Christmas for a new duke who years ago sabotaged her chance for happiness. She quickly falls for the duke's charming but not very competent factor, not knowing that he's hiding something also—he's the duke she despised!

Convincing the Countess

When a business-minded aristocrat encounters a fetching widow he knew years earlier as the bride of a ne'er-do-well earl, temptation steers him along a track that may derail all his plans. Can he convince her to set a course for her future that includes him?

The Impetuous Heiress

Before dashing Lord Loughton can make amends with his neglected fiancée, the lady's meddling cousin delivers her to his doorstep. He soon realizes more is amiss than his carelessness. Can he uncover her secrets and win her back before he loses her altogether?

The Nabob's Designing Daughter

Ripped from his prestigious practice to deliver a Highland duke's heir, a young doctor is anxious to return to London. But more snares await than a risky birth, including a surprise—and worthless—bequest and his best friend's cousin, who's blossomed from mousey to heart-stirringly beautiful, with enough wiles to convince an ambitious man that his heart belongs in the Highlands.

The Macbeth Series

Fated Hearts,

A Love After All Retelling of the Scottish Play

A Scottish Baron returning from two decades at war meets the wife he divorced and the daughter he disavowed before she was born, only to learn that everything he'd believed was a lie. Determined to win back the only woman he's ever loved he must first face the viper who drove them apart.

The Comtesse of Midnight

A Scottish Earl on a quest for the elusive Comtesse de Fontenay, rescues a French lady smuggler during a devastating storm, taking shelter with her. As the stormy night drags on, he suspects she knows the lady he's seeking, the lady who holds the secret to his identity.

Claims of the Heart

Since a perilous fall, Lucie Macbeth has been seeing more than a settled future as the heiress to a Scottish barony. The visions plaguing her include a man—one far above her class and breeding, and English to boot. He's engaged to a duke's granddaughter as well, and thus wholly inappropriate. Though she can't marry him, and she won't become any man's leman, when the Sight warns her of danger to him her conscience, and her heart tell her she can't walk away.

Find excerpts and buy links at https://AlinaKField.com

and sign up for my monthly emails for news about upcoming books and sales.

www.ingramcontent.com/pod-product-compliance
Lightning Source LLC
Chambersburg PA
CBHW071328130626
46556CB00004B/1793